"Lord You Know, and So Does Myrtle"

"LORD YOU KNOW, AND SO DOES MYRTLE"

Approximately 71,466 words

By Stephanie E. Hart

mytimets2@icloud.com
(404)392-4255

ISBN: 9798810861621

Dedication

"Upon my bed of anguish, languish and affliction…Lord, you know.

When I don't know from where, the next piece of bread my children shall eat will come…Lord, you know.

When misunderstood, and all my labor seems in vain…Lord, you know.

When through the fire and through the flood I've come, and I stand unmoved by life's storms…Lord, you alone know."

"I will name a lot of people below. BUT! This first one is for YOU Dee! I believe your siblings can understand why I say and chose to do this."

I dedicate this book to, my Mother, my best earthly friend. Lord, give rest to her beautiful, colorful, soulful soul. Joan Adams George Johnson. She looked to Jesus for EVERYTHING! Because she taught me about Jesus, I knew that I was loved. I dedicate this book to my Sister and spiritual best friend and the Prayer Warrior in our family. Lord, give rest to her beautiful soul. Mary Elizabeth George Morris. These two women taught me sooo much about ME! Also; they taught me how to lean and depend on JESUS! Oh how my heart yearns for the longing of their presence! I dedicate this book to my first (earthly) Loves; my beloved and the reason I breathe, my children. Michael 'Dee' DeWayne George, Lord Chika Onyebueke, Hart Onyebueke, and Rhoda 'Chinasa' Onyebueke; who's responsible for my Foreword...in case you didn't notice lol! Thank you guys for the wonder years and the PUSH that encouraged me to see this through! Thank you for having us, when your siblings were too young to care for themselves Dee. I wasn't strong enough to do it alone. But God gave me you at 15 years young! He rose up a warrior in you Dee! Thank you for never turning your back on us! Thank you for being the wind beneath our wings. I dedicate this book to the one that has been the closest to a Mother to me since my Dear Mother transitioned to her place of rest. Evelyn 'Tiny' Covington Hall, you have shown me loving-kindness, companionship, care, wisdom, favor and strength when I was weary of trying to do it without Mama. Thank you Auntie Tiny. To my aunties, Helen, Yvonne, Dorothia, Connie, Elsie, Duffy, Merna, Alfreda ‘Peanut’, and Cousin Rhonda thank you for being kind and supportive to me and my siblings through the years. I dedicate this book to my Daddy, John Henry Johnson. He's not down here after the others because he is less vital to my life. No, he's the one that was THERE! He is the kindest and most patient and sacrificing dad that we could have asked for. He is STILL there for us! We don't call him "Step Dad". He is Dad! I love you Johnny. Thank you from the bottom of my heart for taking care of Mama and her 5 children the way you did. You certainly didn't have to. But, you chose to. I dedicate this book to my two younger sisters, Shelia George Jackson, who keeps me laughing and praying! Thank you Curtland 'Pepper' Jackson, and Shelia for carrying me and my Kids when Mama left, and we had to return home. To Tanya Watson, who has believed in me when I didn't even believe in myself! Thank you for the financial support to this project when it was still on the cold slab of desire only. Thank you for "Getting Me", or else, how could you do "About the Author" for me? I dedicate this book to my Big brother, King Michael George! This Jovial, 'Quiet Storm' of the family! Thank you for being ***my best*** male friend Michael. We mirror each other in so many things in our personality and I like that! I dedicate this book to my beautiful, JOYS, Landyn, Michael, Deondre, Messiah, Makai, and Audriana Rose! Thank You Kellie, Tori and Nikki for giving me these treasures that give me a delight ***every time*** they call me "Mimi"! I dedicate this book to my nephews. These warrior kings have all had my back in their own capacity of love for me and mine. Jermaine, I see ya! Proud of you King! Fredravis…, you already know! May God bless you a hundred fold in return! Thank you! Shannon…, you too! Thank you! Corey, my spiritual joy in the Lord, and jack of all trades, with the gift of Art in those ***blessed*** hands of yours! The hands that illustrated the background art on the cover of my first Novel! I am very proud and privileged to have your GIFT representing for ME! Leonard thank you for being there for my 3 younger ones in Georgia…even today, you still extend your kindness. Terrell, you give the best hugs! Of course that's after my grandbaby Dre, Lol. God has his hand on you. Desmond, I see you trying and so does God. They tell me that you are my child, and Hart is Shelia's. Well, you can be mine too. But, I won't give my Hart to anyone! Aaron, you and Mike Jr. already know that you two have my heart! To my nieces, Jessmine 'Punky', and Michaela 'Red', I love you beautiful princesses! To my great nieces and nephews the abundances of favor, blessings, and God's protection and keeping, all the days of your lives. To my pastor and friend, Pamela Drumgole, a woman of thunder and integrity, and a heart filled with the love and compassion of God for people. She has been so THERE for me when I needed her! The many prayers, instruction, wisdom and truth about me, both good, and bad made all of the difference. Apostle Johnny Drumgole and Dr. Pamela Cage Drumgole and the pastoral team of Liberty Christian Center, of Monroe, Winnsboro, and Arcadia, Louisiana, have been so instrumental in my walk in the Lord! I would be remiss if I failed to acknowledge my first daddy in the WORD, Pastor Donald Franklin, and his wife Pastor Audrenia Franklin! They taught me so much about Holy Spirit and the Righteousness of God that I am...IN CHRIST JESUS! I dedicate this book to a few women that I have held near and dear to my heart from childhood, and up to this moment. To my newest, faithful, classy, loving, and truly God fearing dear friend, Sarah Banks! From childhood, Loretha Robinson, my sister from another mother, and precious friend of 50 plus years! DeWanna 'Dee'

Williams Greer, my childhood next door neighbor and dear family friend of over 50 years as well! To Carolyn Ford, I have known her for 40 years now. We get on the phone after not talking for many moons and it feels like we just talked yesterday! Thank you, Carolyn for always making time for me. I learned a lot of life lessons from the funny things you shared your view points about when I would call you with matters of the heart, or if I just needed a friend in the moments of my hard places. Michelle Dollar, whom I feel the MOST at home in my skin with. My prayer partner, and the first person I met when moving to a big, unfamiliar city. She took me by the hand and showed me love, the ropes, and how to breast feed my daughter, and how to STAND. Thank you, Michelle. Geraldine McGee, I don't know how I would've made it through my College days without you Geraldine! It's not many that you can trust with your babies. Geraldine was there to help me with care for my baby boys at the time when I needed someone so badly! She had a hot cup of Coffee waiting for me when I brought them through on my way to school, ***every*** morning! She had an encouraging word and some laughter to share with me. She did it most times for no pay at all! She loved me and my boys when it was needed it most! Thank you Geraldine! We had some powerful prayer times together more than anything! Sheryl Maddox, Angela Hughes, Mary Cegaye, you ladies have been my leaning post! Patricia 'Pat' Walton, Danielle 'Sassy' Curry, Sariyah 'Them hands' Moore and Marsha Carter (my Georgia Peach girls), whom each one has a piece of my heart in their own individual, special way. To Wilma George, my Sister -in -Love, Victoria Matthews Morris, Donna Wallace and last but certainly not least, Pastor JoAnn F Tyson and Joanne Scott. These Queens from Monroe, La. RIGHT HERE! They have had my back, and front, when some people in my own family didn't even know that I was going through! I love you ladies and thank you for the years. This is to the Mothers, Wives and Daughters, Girlfriends, and Sisters, to those that hold the hands and heartstrings of one another. To those that, through like passions, journeys and struggles, that have to concede and say, "Through my frail places, my weakness and ignorance, I have learned…when I don't know…Lord, YOU know!

Lord You Know and So Does Myrtle

Acknowledgements

Tanya Watson: About the Author/Investor
Chinasa Onyebueke: Foreword/Investor
Michael DeWayne George: Investor
Lord Onyebueke: Investor
Hart Onyebueke: Investor
Fredravis George: Investor
Shannon George: Investor
Aaron Morris: Investor
Shelia Jackson: Investor
*Corey Abrums George: Illustrator of Front and Back Background Cover Art foundation
Muhammad Kaleem @rock_0407 on Fiverr: Designer of Book Cover graphics

Author Tiffany Anderson
Author Stephanie Oliver
Author Chanda Ford
Author Shunda Brown
Author Fred Jones
Author Shannon McMurray

Encouraging words and prayers from:
Michael Wayne George
Shelia Jackson
LaTonya 'Nikki' Benton
Victoria Bowker

Evelyn “Tiny” Covington Hall
Constance Hawthorne Robinson
Victoria Matthew Morris
Donna Wallace
Marsha Carter Amode

Ladies of Legacy Hair Salon:
Sariyah Moore Owner/Operator
Adonica
Amber
Angie
Annette Tako
Apryl
Asma
Audriana
Becky
Breezy
Carolyn Haygood
Chinasa
Courtney
Dodie Minor
Donna
Jadean
Ivy Durham
Jasmine/Stephanie
Jennifer and Jade
Katelynn
Kaylee
Kemaye
Jaida
Lucinta
Madison
Michelle Simpson
Michelle Jones
Neekthehairgeek
Nicole Holley
Rita Nwanjoku
Shawndya
Shay

Tedra
Tiffany
Ursla
Yanii

For every gesture of kindness, push, critique, or support offered; THANK YOU KINDLY!!
For those that I failed to mention; there are more than I can name. Over the years, you guys have been instrumental in some big or small way. Please know that I really do appreciate your place in my journey with this labor of LOVE.

*Corey George, I ESPECIALLY thank you!! You go wayyyy back with me on this work! I remember when I first told you about it. You were my first cheering squad! You offered your help before you even knew what or how I wanted to get it done. Many moons later; you're ***still*** rooting me on! You DID that work of beautiful Tapestry on the front and back of the Cover! May God cause your GIFT to make room for you, and bring you before Kings, and great men and women! Keep on creating Nephew!

Foreword

"Lord You Know and So Does Myrtle" is a project that I have watched my mother build into a beautiful story that is now in your hands to read. I have always enjoyed hearing my mom tell stories about her childhood and what things were like "back in her day." If you know my mom, you know she has some of the best stories and she will tell it with so much detail and emotion that you felt like you were there witnessing it yourself. When she asked me to write this foreword, I was enamored with many emotions. Pride is what I felt the most. To see the struggles that she went through behind completing this book and now to see it finally come to fruition just made me feel so proud of her! She has faced many obstacles along the way, such as losing everything in a house fire… yes, *everything* including her original draft of this book. However, with so much discouragement she was still determined to share this phenomenal story.

My mom has always been fascinated with Crepe Myrtles and their colorful blooms and shapes and sizes of the trees. Every time I see a crepe myrtle I think of my mom. It is said that many cultures believe that cultivating a crepe myrtle will bring love and peace to your family. While Monia's family is far from your typical "peaceful" family, there is no denying their sacrificial love for each other.

My mom grew up in Louisiana and if you know anything about the South, then you will understand the Southern 'twang' throughout this story. She wanted to tell her story *exactly* how it was growing up in the projects in Louisiana where there were a plethora of personalities, grown folks (sometimes-even children) cussed, and Ebonics was everyone's first language. Do not mind the grammatical errors as it is intended to prescribe to the habit of speaking that was accustomed to growing up in the projects. As you make your way through this page-turner, you will laugh, you will cry, and you will feel all of the flavor and spirit of the South, according to her recollection. I know you will enjoy this book as much as the author, my mom, enjoyed writing it for you all.

Chinasa Onyebueke
4/08/2022

Preface

When initially deciding to take on the task of getting this particular piece out to the public, family and friends; I was writing to get off some steam. I considered that, kids of this era just don't know how to have fun like we did as children. Then, the nostalgia set in. I needed to do something with the many thoughts and imaginations swirling around in my head. I wondered if I could tell it like I remembered things were in my generation. I thought about the games we played and the music of that time, the spirit of family and community…good and bad. I did not know when I picked up my Laptop that it would lead me here. I started writing this work way back in 2005! I had a number of setbacks to take place. But, I was determined. See, as a young girl, I would sit in my bedroom while the other kids were out playing. I would just be writing poetry, and listening to the radio. Each time that I finished a piece, I would ball it up and get rid of it because, I didn't want anyone to discover the matters of my heart and what I thought was corny and naïve thoughts at that time. How I wished that I hadn't done that now. Life has taught me many lessons. Come to think about it now, those writings were not so corny after all. I see that a lot of the flavor of those poems and love letters and talks with God back then, really are the heart of this story. Let me say this; I know that there will be those that read it and find places of confusion about a couple of things said here. Some may even question my spirituality, and my position on a couple of matters mentioned here. I expected as much. I am only here to deliver a message of Love, Acceptance, and to provoke each reader to consider his fellow man. I don't have the yardstick of standard for anyone. I am only sharing a story with a message of Redemption and I

believe it will hit each person that reads it where they have lived, are living, or will live at some juncture in their journey in this place. For the cussing that goes on here, I used to be a strong cusser! I got redeemed. For the drinking, partying, fighting, smoking, drugging, you name it! I did it, or tried it! Guess what? I got redeemed! I believe if you look really close, between the mirror, and this storyline, you just may find yourself in this story somewhere. Remember, it's not a story of Judgment, or to be critical of ANYONE. It's only intended to entertain and provoke thoughts, memories, and offer a message of Hope and Redemption to those that realize the need or desire for it. I hope you laugh, I hope it inspires you to get to know your Creator more intimately. I really hope it inspires you to take pen to paper and your fingers to the keyboard to tell some of the stuff that's been spinning around in your brilliant minds. Thank you for choosing to purchase your copy of my first Novel of hopefully, many more works to come. I thoroughly enjoyed writing it and I must admit that, I had to laugh at myself sometimes! Holy Spirit is indeed the Great Teacher! I don't know what I would have done without his direction, and Great Grace! Just as Chinasa Onyebueke said in the Foreword; the grammatical errors are intended, as to depict the general conversation and characteristics of the typical dialogue between the people of that community and time. When I said that I had to laugh at myself sometimes, I meant that. Because, I can speak that same Ebonics, and jump straight "Proper" in the blink of an eye!
A word from the author,

Ms. Stephanie Hart
04//2022

"Lord, where's Dummy?"

I knew that morning when I woke up, it was gonna be a crazy day. I didn't wet the bed; I fell out of the bed! That's what woke me up! I was in the room alone. That certainly was weird. I usually had to crawl over Sasha, and Sharletta to get out. It was a crazy quiet in the house! I gathered myself from the floor, went to pee a river because, my bladder was full from not wetting the bed. When I came to the front of the house, no one was in the living room, or the kitchen. I went out the door to see where everyone was. Several people were gathered in different circles. Some with their heads dropped not saying anything. Some were crying that silent cry we cry when we are too heavy inside to let it out without losing it. That's the look I saw on mama's face. I ran to her to see what the matter was. When she saw me, it got worse. Everyone was looking at me like they all were keeping some great secret from me. I looked at them, then to mama. No one said a word! I began to pull mama by the hand away from everyone. I felt I needed to ask her in secret what was going on. She sat me down on the stoop and put her hand, gently on my face. I knew then, it had something to do with me, and would hurt me. I just started shaking my head. That helped me to block out what she was about to say. She put both of her hands on my face then. I could see around her that everyone was watching us. In my mind, I made myself to look straight past them into NO WHERE. Whatever it was….I just didn't want to know.

Table of Contents

Chapter 1

Why All of the Tears?

"Mama, why you crying?" "Gone child, go somewhere and play!" She snapped at me. Something on the inside of me quaked! So; I did what was natural for me when stuff like that happened. I ran out the front door, pounced up the Crepe Myrtle with the swiftness of a cat! I would climb to the highest branch of the tree, the one that would support my weight, and would hide me from the view of everybody else in the crowded house I lived in as a child. I don't even think crowded is the right word for it. There were 3 sisters, with 11 children between them, a grandmother, and a rabbit named Marty, in a 3 bedroom, one bathroom apartment, in the projects of New Roads, Louisiana! That tree was my place of retreat, and refuge. That tree was the place where I did all of my thinking, crying, and praying. Yes, I learned at an early age that I could carry my cares, fears, and dreams to my creator. That tree was the place I ran to when the chaos or the events of the day inside of the house made me feel like I was suffocating! My grandma planted that tree, and the huge, Magnolia that stood across the yard from my sanctuary. I loved being there because I could smell the blossoms of the Magnolia, spy on the goings and comings of the neighbors, and cry, without anybody knowing it. I just wish I knew why I was crying?

I knew something was wrong, because my first grade teacher came by our house, and she left crying as well! I was already shaking in my bones when I saw her pull up. I couldn't figure what I'd done on Friday, for mama to be getting a visit on early Saturday morning! I hid out as much as possible. Everyone else was watching cartoons, and eating breakfast. My grandmother always knew where to find me. I think she liked the fact that I got so much enjoyment from my time in that tree. She even made a point to keep the other kids from getting in the tree to bother me. We had this little bond about the tree between us. She didn't say it; but I knew she held that special place in her heart that felt really good that I got so much fulfillment from being in that tree she planted, before I was even born! She didn't insist that I come down for breakfast with the other kids this particular morning. My grandma came out of the house with the broom, as it was her routine to do. She went to sweeping the front porch off, humming, and looking about the block to see who was doing what that morning. When she knew she had my attention, and no one else's....she started talking as if, to herself. "You know, Mrs. Tyler must be crazy to think that Jazzy was gone give her daughter to her to keep! She done come over here and got Jazzy, and herself all worked up for nothing. Um huh, that's what she did. Sheen know, Jazzy don't play 'bout huh chilren!" As fast as I climbed that Crepe Myrtle, I was down to the ground to see what grandma was talking about! I didn't say a word. I just gave her that knowing look that let her know that I understood, and, I wouldn't say a word about what she had just said. I gave her that look to see if she would confirm what I thought I had heard her say, without saying it. She just grunted, kept sweeping, and said, "Humph, sho did!"

I eased back into the house to see if everything had quieted down. Everyone was looking at me like I was the red headed step-child. They knew something that I didn't. But, no one dared to say a word! Mama was in the bathroom, washing her face I would guess. I listened to see what I could hear. Just as I moved in closer....just about to put my ear to the door...she yanked it open! I fell, face first into the bathroom! She never looked back to see if I was ok, or to get onto me about being nosy, and spying on her. She just marched down the hall to the kitchen, and started banging pots and pans around, and hollering to the other gazillion kids to bring their cereal bowls to the kitchen! I got up, marched right back out to my tree. I knew I had better stay out of the way.

Sunday came. We did our regular routine of getting ready for church. The deacons did their extremely long devotionals as the choir and congregation heemed and hawed the "Doctor Watts", old Negro spirituals. There was one that always moved me to tears. Lydia was the lead singer in the choir. She had a tenor range that sent chills through you when she sang! She bellowed out… "If the Lord don't help me…I can't stand the storms!" Then we would join in to follow her lead. Man; that did something in my little soul! I knew that all we had in the projects was the storms of life! The Lord had to sho nuff help us!

Sunday dinner was so good! If you don't believe nothing else I tell you; please believe this: My grandma and her daughters could cook their wigs off! **We ate good**! Each of the sisters got Food stamps, and my auntee (that's how we said it in the south) worked at the local grocery store. She knew when all of the meat specials were going on. After all of the Ham, Cheese Potatoes, Green Beans, (filled with bacon) and dinner rolls, not to mention, the Banana Pudding that mama made…we were full, bellies fat, and all ready for a nap! That was the nap of all naps on Sunday, after church, and Sunday dinner. Of course, me and Sasha had to get our usual whipping before we got off to sleep. We had to squabble over something. Anything would do. I really believe that we did this so we could get that one whipping that made you cry, and rock yourself to sleep, feeling sorry for yourself. Sasha would actually lie there and count the welts she had received! This time there was something different about this whipping. Mama didn't hit me as hard, or as many times as she normally would. In my mind, I was almost sure it had to do with whatever had happened on Saturday's visit from Mrs. Tyler. I was just overjoyed about it, whatever the reason was.

Monday morning came too quickly! I was already nervous about going to face Mrs. Tyler after the events of the past weekend. Somebody please….help me spell awkward! That wasn't even a strong enough word to describe how I felt when I walked into the classroom that gloomy, Monday morning.

I recall how hard it was for me to learn to read in first grade. I was so timid then! It also didn't help that I was so intrigued with my teacher that I couldn't even concentrate on the lesson! She was so beautiful! I would pay attention to every detail of her doings. The way she walked with such grace thru the aisles as she passed out our books. The way she wrote on the chalk board, or read a story to us, and at end of the day, how she gathered up the materials, and placed everything in a *just so* manner.

I was raised to obey my elders, and don't talk back, or ask a whole bunch of questions of adults. Mrs. Tyler, told me to gather my things because I would be going home with her that evening. I'm thinking, she was giving me a ride home. I didn't question her. I just got my stuff together like she told me to. All of the kids rolled their eyes at me when I got into her big, fine, Old's 98. I was nervous, proud, and felt like the most important kid in the school! The smell on the inside was like fresh linen off the clothes line, and a hint of whatever the fragrance was that she wore. We didn't have a car at that time. So; I knew I'd better make this cruise past the kids look good! I waved at them like I thought I was the 'Queen of the School'! I got all sorts of mean glares from them. I didn't care. I felt special. I tried to behave like I road in a fine car all of the time. She didn't say a word. She just let me enjoy the moment. I thought she was giving me a ride home. Not so. As we started taking a route I was not familiar with. I got a little nervous. She must've sensed it. She started to explain that I was to come over to her place that evening and, I would come to school from there in the morning. All sorts of thoughts went through my head. She still kept quiet.

As we rounded the corner to come into her neighborhood, I thought I was coming into the white folk's neighborhood. You have to understand.... I had only been out of my hood, which was "The Hood", only at Christmas time to go see the lights in the White Folk community. Even then, it was dark. So; to be strolling up in this nice car, into this fabulous place was like Christmas day to me all over again! She could tell I was amazed. I was looking to the left, and the right, and all over the back seat to see the nice houses we passed up! She just smiled.

By the time we got to her house, I didn't think there could be that many nice homes left to view, because my little neck was tired from stretching and flexing already! Boy; was I wrong! We pulled up to what I thought was the White House! She just wheeled into the circular drive in front like it was no big deal! I was looking for servants to come out and meet us! Instead, there were two of the most handsome boys I had ever laid my eyes on! Robby and Jeremy I learned. Robby was tall, lanky, and a beautiful, cinnamon complexion, with big dreamy eyes. Even with his glasses on...he was still gorgeous! Jeremy, Jeremy, Jeremy! He was an exact replica of his mother! I thought she was beautiful! He was the epitome of a Greek god! He was a smooth, golden complexion. He had very serious, strong, sculptured features. His nostrils flared when he laughed, or got excited. You could see his excitement when he saw me. Yep, at 6 years old…I could tell when someone was excited to see me. It gave me Goosebumps when he smiled at me. He was very muscular for an eight year old boy! His mom noticed the vibe between us. She made a point to distract him by telling him to get her things out of the back seat of the car. Robby was the perfect gentleman. He immediately took my books from me and proceeded to take me into the house. We went into the area that was her sewing room. It was huge, and orderly. The French doors were something new to me. They gave way to the rest of the house. As we entered the kitchen, I could smell something very delicious going on in there. There stood a very tall man with a smile that warmed the whole house! Mr. Tyler. I was made to think twice about Jeremy looking so like his mom when I saw Mr. Tyler. The smile, the flare of the nostrils was every bit of where Jeremy got his features.

This man was cooking up a meal to make any woman think twice about whether she could truly cook or not. He was cooking, Collard greens, Pork chops, candied Yams, Corn on the cob, and Hot Water cornbread as we called it in the dirty south! I was starving, but too shame faced to admit it when he asked me if I wanted something to eat. Mrs. Tyler told him that was the craziest question she had ever heard. She reminded him of how hungry the boys were when they came home from school. She didn't ask me if I was hungry, or ready to eat. She just told me to go wash up for dinner, pointed out where I was to sit and started fixing my plate. I noticed she sat me in the chair next to her but she was between me and Jeremy.

Robby was just genuinely friendly, and helpful. I always ate as slow as a snail, and I still eat as slow as a snail to this day. Robby stayed at the table with me until I finished, and I was embarrassed for him to watch me eat. So, he turned sideways in his chair, and talked to me about everything, and everybody in the neighborhood to watch out for. I wondered why he told me this because I figured I was only going to be over there for the night, and off to school the next day. I finally finished eating and that's when I got the tour of the rest of the house. It was awesome! Everything made sense to me when I was introduced to a room that was called MY ROOM. It was completely done in white and pink, and lavender. It had a full sized, white canopy bed, laced with a pink, sheer canopy over it. There were dolls, teddy bears, a toy chest, and a white rocking chair with a book shelf beside it. I also learned why I didn't need to go home first for any clothing, because, the closet was filled with clothes just for me, already! I was, confused. If all of this was for me…and this was MY ROOM….what about my things, and MY ROOM at home with my mama, and sisters and brother, and cousins and nem? Mrs. Tyler stood at the doorway and watched for my reaction to everything with a look of pride and joy in her eyes. That is, until she saw the confusion in my eyes. She came over and sat on the bed beside me, and asked me if I liked it. I just nodded my head up and down. She asked me what was wrong. I told her I wanted to talk to my mama. She said that would be fine. She asked me if I liked the dolls and the clothes in the closet. I asked her why there were so many? She laughed at me. I guess nobody ever complained about having too many nice clothes. That's when she began to explain that those clothes and this room was for the time that I would be coming over to be with her and the boys sometimes so she could help my mama with me. I told her my mama didn't need no help with me; she was doing a good job already. She began to put it another way, by showing me how the crowded conditions in our project home was making it hard for my mama to keep us comfortable and she was going to let me have this room when I needed to get away from all of that. I told her that I went to my tree when I felt crowded. She didn't know about the tree, and I felt a bit mad with myself because I made mention of it to her. That was me and my grandma's secret. She came from another angle. It would help mama to provide better for me by being over there with these things until she could get a bigger place for just us. Of course, I had an answer back. I had to make her see that I loved my cousins, and grandma being there with us. I had to show her that I really liked everything in the room; I just didn't want to have to leave my family.

Even as a child my mind was able to imagine how my mama must've felt to know that there was someone that was able to provide for me what she couldn't at the time. I knew she must be feeling afraid that this woman would somehow win me over to want to come live with her so I could have all of the stuff that little girls dream about. Well, my heart was fixed. I had so much love and adoration from my mama that, I saw past the beauty of Mrs. Tyler's world, and wanted what really made my life a happy place. That was the place of Family love. We slept 3 deep in the bed of a crowded room. We fought our sisters and brothers, and cousins. Mama and her sisters even fought sometimes! I'm talking, throwing some serious blows! They would be biting, kicking, hair pulling, and clawing! But, nobody in the hood better ever be found trying to bother either one of the children at 49A Redan Drive!

Chapter 2

Pissy Me!

Mrs. Tyler's reason for being there that Saturday became clear to me when I got home. I eased back to mama's room, and stood in the doorway, as quiet as a church house mouse. Mama was drying her tears, and looking around for her cigarettes. When she saw me standing there…she beckoned for me to come sit by her on the bed. I sat there silently, and she was too for a moment. "You love your mama don't you baby?" It seemed as if she was answering her own question as she was asking it kinda. I said… "I sure do." She began to enquire about my visit with Mrs. Tyler. I spoke of the nice neighborhood, the nice house she lived in, the nice family, and the place she said was MY ROOM. I told her of all the toys, and clothes, and the beautiful bed in MY ROOM. I could see a hint of fear in her eyes. I assured her that none of those things mattered to me if I wouldn't be able to have her and my family anymore. She started crying again, and so did I. We just hugged each other and cried for a little while as she rocked me from side to side there on the side of her bed.

She cleared her throat, blew her nose, and dried her tears and mine. She told me Mrs. Tyler always wanted a daughter, but couldn't have more kids. That's why she wanted mama to give me to her. I was sad for her. Then I understood why she left the house running and crying. Mama had told her she couldn't adopt me. Jazzy had a heart of gold though. She made a compromise with me and Mrs. Tyler. I could; only if I wanted to, go stay with her during the summer for a couple of weeks," just to make her feel better". Then, when it was time to start preparing for school again… I could come home and be with her and the rest of the family.

I was a bed wetter then. My biggest fear was what would happen if I peed in that pretty bed?! Well, I got the chance to find out. The time came when I was to go to the Tyler's. Mama told me that I could call her anytime I wanted to, and I could come home anytime I felt I was ready to. That was all I needed to hear. I knew I was gonna miss out on all the fun of the Projects, all the block parties the big kids had, and all the laughs we got when JoJo and L.B. came to the house to hang with Jazzy and Tee nem. These two cats were flaming sissies! They weren't trying to be in the closet about it at all! They babysat for mama when she and her sisters wanted to go out clubbing. We had the time of our lives when they were around! They cooked the best food, combed our hair, let us play dress up with them, in all of the pretty dresses and robes mama had gotten from overseas when our dad was away in the military. We played jacks with them, they hipped us to the latest dance moves, and L.B. could sang his butt off! JoJo was the drum major for the high school band. They were some nuts! Mama knew we were in good hands with them though. They loved us, and would fight at the drop of a hat! L. B. started talking to me about my going away for the summer. I confided in him that I was afraid of peeing in that pretty bed. "Hell, if it's good enough for you to piss in Jazzy's bed, then its damned well alright to piss in Mrs. Tyler's beds at her house!" JoJo agreed wholeheartedly as he twisted his lips to the side, rolled his neck, and walled his eyes. That's the instruction that I got about that. I went on to playing with my cousins.

Saturday came. I left my tree, my mama, and family, and headed to the Tyler's house for the summer. Mrs. Tyler and the boys came to pick me up. You should've seen the looks on my sister and cousin's faces when they saw Robby, and Jeremy! My big sister Miriam yanked me by the arm and warned me not to be over there being fast with them manish tail boys! I had to remind her that I wasn't even thinking 'bout no manish boys! That is, except Jeremy maybe. You know I kept that part to myself.

Mama kept her head up high, and kept that look that said strength to me in her eyes. She hugged me, kissed me on the forehead, and winked at me. It always did something for me when mama would wink at me. It let me know she believed in me, and we had that little signal between us. I could leave now with peace.

Mrs. Tyler had a spring in her step and a smile of love in her eyes towards mama. They whispered something among themselves. Robby was busy trying to get my bags to the car. Even though I had everything I could imagine needing at the Tyler's….mama's pride insisted that I had my own panties, and pj's, her favorite hair bows for me, and the hand-made rag doll from my grandma was my pride and joy. All was set. I was going to help bring joy to Mrs. Tyler, and….find out what makes Jeremy tick.

On the ride over, I was curious to learn about all of the stuff they did for fun in the neighborhood. Robby gave me a rundown of what appeared to make for a boring summer. They played touch football when they weren't working in the woods lumberjacking with their dad. This explained why Jeremy was so chiseled and why they both had such burnished complexions. Mr. Tyler looked just like a black Paul Bunion! He was a tall burly, but handsome as all get out kind of man! He had a very hearty laugh, and a very pleasant disposition. I soon felt drawn to him. I would always rat on the boys for the least little thing. Just so I could get the attention Mr. Tyler gave me.

It was safe to say that it felt good to have the safety and support of a daddy figure around me. Mr. Tyler would create situations to get on the boys about me. Mrs. Tyler would just give me that knowing look and shake her head, and stay out of it. You could tell that I was bringing a lot of joy to her world. This made me feel important. When I noticed her looking at me from across the room with wonder in her eyes that Sunday morning after I got there…I could tell she was thinking what it would be like to have her own little girl. My heart began to ache for her for a while. I think she knew that I knew.

Well, I peed in the pretty bed. It was so weird. I dreamt that I was on the toilet at my house in the Projects. I was sooo sleepy as I sat there on the toilet! It felt so good! There's nothing like the feeling of relieving yourself on your own toilet at HOME! All of a sudden! I felt really cold! The kind of cold that shocks you back to reality! I jumped up! Ohh no! Not in the pretty bed! What to do??! I had to think fast! I must've pissed a river! It was all up my back, down my legs, and the mattress was soaked! I started pulling sheets and trying to figure out why I had to pee again! The fear of what was gonna happen next made me feel the need to run and pee again! Everyone was sound asleep. I thought. Not Jeremy. Of all the people on the planet…why did he have to spot me soaking wet, running to the bathroom as he was coming out of it! I pushed past him, and got some on him! It was on! He pushed me as hard as he could into the door post! BAM! It knocked the wind out of me, and made me forget about peeing again. All that registered in my mind was…Kill him! The many Project fights with the boys, and cousins welled up in my mind! I was taught that you don't worry if you can beat them, you just get yo respect! That's exactly what I proceeded to do. I didn't remember the crush I had on him. I didn't care about trying to go hide the sheets in the closet, nor the fact that we were gonna wake up the whole house! I only knew that I had to show him that he couldn't handle me like that! I lit into him so fast, he didn't know whether the blows I delivered him or the pissiness I put all over him hurt the worst!

Well; everyone was awake at that point. I think Mrs. Tyler had second thoughts about me being the daughter she always wanted when she saw the football hold I was taught by my big brother, pinning her son down! Just another boy in her mind! Mr. Tyler grabbed me and pried me off of Jeremy, stood him to his feet, and Jeremy began to rip his clothes off! They all thought he had lost his mind! He yelled, "Yuck, she got her pee all over me!" All eyes were on me now. Mrs. Tyler was looking at me dumbfounded. I was still huffing and puffing with my eyes to the ground. Jeremy took a dive for the bathtub to get it off of him. None of the craziness that we ever did in my house could compare with that night. My secret was out. Robby felt so sorry for me. Mrs. Tyler marched me into the room to see what had happened in there. I started trying to gather the sheets up so it wouldn't look so bad. She gently pulled them from my arms, and said, "It's ok honey, it's just a bed." I started crying, with so many mixed emotions about it all. I wondered how she could be such a sweet woman to feel like this. I not only peed all over a brand new mattress, and nice sheets, but…I had also, beat the brakes off of her son, and woke the whole house up in the middle of the night! I was confused because she showed the same kind of love to me that my own mama had when I wet the bed. I was at a loss of how to feel about her. I didn't want to see her the same way I saw my mama. I felt like I would be cheating on my mom!

In the meantime; Mr. Tyler was scolding Jeremy for letting a girl whip his ass! That's the first time I ever heard a curse word in their house! I was shocked! Yet; it was kinda cool to be bragged on, in a twisted kind of way. Jeremy was trying to plead his case. He tried to paint a picture of me sneaking him as he came out of the bathroom. That didn't help. It led to questions about why we were up together that time of night in the first place! Mrs. Tyler asked the same thing of me. I had to go through all of the stuff about my dream of being on the toilet…up to that moment. All of them, including Jeremy, laughed me to shame! I was confused again! How could they be laughing when I had caused so much trouble? Mr. Tyler was trying to explain it all. I was like, "Ohh!" We all laughed and, I got a bath and had to sleep on the sofa in the den until the mattress situation was dealt with. That being, I got a new mattress. Just like that! I was sure these people were rich! At my house, mama just placed the mattress on the back porch until it dried, and covered it with plastic, and told me that I was not gonna get anymore Kool Aid at night until I learned to stop peeing in the bed. The new mattress was covered in a nice, zip up cover when it came. Mrs. Tyler told me to try and get up at night when I felt I had to pee, and go to the bathroom. If I couldn't make it, she would understand. Boy, this family was great! I thought that until Jeremy started acting ugly to me, on the regular! Robby, on the other hand, was just smothering me with niceness. It was going fine until I was picked one time too many by the other cute guy in the neighborhood. Justin was cute, but not as cute as Jeremy. Justin liked the way I played football just like the boys. This led to me always being picked to be on his team. Jeremy didn't like all of the attention I was getting from Justin. I loved this! It made me think that Jeremy was really into me. When the game was over, and everybody had gone home…I had to deal with Jeremy acting cold and obnoxious with me. If I walked too close to him down the hall, he went out of the way to make sure I didn't brush up on him. He didn't show any table manners towards me, and he didn't talk to me anymore. I tried to act as if it didn't bother me, but that was my first, official, puppy love, heartache. I knew Mr. Tyler was onto us. He stopped me from playing football with the boys, and he went out of the way to make mention that we were just as well brothers and sisters because we would be spending our summers together from now on! I was ready to go home at that point. I couldn't imagine not being with my family every summer! I wanted to call mama then. I waited until Mrs. T was coming to talk with me before bed, like she did each night. That's when I asked her if what Mr. T said was true? She wanted to know how I felt about it. I had to be honest, and quickly. I let her know that I didn't feel that I would like it if I had to be away from my family every summer. She assured me that we would just take things one summer at a time. The other side of the thing was, I didn't want to be like a sister to Jeremy. My childhood fantasy was, this boy is gonna be my husband one day, and we were gonna live just like Mr. and Mrs. Tyler, and I was gonna act just like my mama, Jazzy when I grew up! So, why was Mr. T trying to change my future?! I started pulling away from him. Things started getting awkward for me around them. Robby, was a constant reminder of what I wanted the least. He was always nice, he tried to comfort me each time he knew I was down in the dumps, and, I didn't want that from him, I wanted that from Jeremy! I was really missing my tree! I needed to go up there so I could cry about Jeremy, and think about this entire brother, sister thing that was going totally against my plans!

Chapter 3

"Dummy"

Mama was so excited to hear from me, and I was more excited to talk to her! She tried to play cool about it so I wouldn't feel like she wanted me to come home. As I talked to her, I learned that she had been talking to Mrs. Tyler about the things that were going on from time-to-time. She knew about the fight with me and Jeremy! She joked with me about whipping his butt. She told me to keep up the good work in defending myself. Her words to her girls were to always keep up a good bluff, and never let a guy see you sweat with fear. I thank her for that today. It helped me to deal with the bullies in the Project. And it helped me to keep a strong face when all the while Jeremy's treatment was breaking my heart. But, he would never know it if I had anything to say about it. I was trying to talk in parables to her to find out why boys acted a certain way with you? She knew right away that I was talking about me liking Jeremy. I was trying to figure out how she always knew these things?! Gosh, I couldn't keep ***nothing*** from her! Not to mention…my auntee Nadine was over there when I was talking to her about it! She was a mess!

She is a story that's not for the faint of heart. Nadine, said what she meant, and meant what she said. That's why her and Jazzy were the best of friends. Mama was considered the "City Girl" to Nadine, and she was the "Flat Foot, Country Gal". They both were the life of the party. They both raised Hell when they had to. They both made no apologies for what their convictions were, and didn't care who agreed with them or not. They would go to the wire for their kids, and they didn't care if they had partied all weekend; they were gonna see to us getting to church on Sundays! Nadine snatched the phone from mama mid-sentence! "Look here lil Heffa, you bet not be over there letting that manish ass boy up in yo draws!" I wasn't even surprised by it. She would take us fishing with her on Saturday mornings, and preach to us the whole time about all boys wanted from us. According to her, "All these damned boys got on their mind is, getting in your draws I tell ya!" Yep, she put it across as raw as she needed to, to make her point of full effect! Mama took the phone back from Nadine, covered the phone and said something I couldn't hear. If, I knew Jazzy like I felt I did....she was cussing Nadine out for saying all of that to me. She went on to find out how my stay was going. I tried to ask her without sounding too sad in front of Mrs. T, when it would be a good time to come over and see my brother, sisters, and cousins? She reminded me of our conversation that day on her bedside. That said to me...anytime I wanted to. So; that's what I did.

I came home for the weekend, and discovered an unusual new friend. Everybody called him "Dummy". He could not hear, and all he could do is grunt, and gesture. I believe he must've been about 20 plus. That's why I said an "Unusual friend". I had played so hard that day that I was exhausted! It was so great to be home, I wasn't sure I would hold up my end of the bargain to just let Mrs. Tyler have some time to love me too.

I was lying there by the window, close to sundown. I was trying to drift off for a bit, but it wasn't working. I guess, I was just too excited about all of the events of the day. I got the chance to play football with the boys in my hood again, I played jumping rope, hopscotch, jacks and "Mother may I" with my sister's and cousins. Man! All the stories everyone told of who had fought with who, and who got the best of who. All of the dance contests at the block parties I'd missed. Then, I heard that, JoJo, and L.B. had beaten the socks off of the neighborhood bully! I was about to die laughing at how my big sister described all the blows they put upside this dude's head! Miriam, my oldest sister was so close with these guys, because they would teach her all of the majorette moves to prepare her for her high school try outs. I liked easing up to listen in on their conversations. JoJo and L. B. knew the low down on everybody that was somebody!

As I was lying there…the face of a crying man was right before my eyes! It would normally have freaked me out, but, he was crying so pitifully that I jumped up to go get Jazzy. She dropped what she was doing, and went out to see what was wrong with him. I wondered why he sounded like he did when he cried. My question was answered when I saw mama, doing all of these different hand signals to him. He was a Mute! I watched in amazement as mama was able to reason with him what the matter was. He explained to her that the kids over on the church yard had thrown rocks and bottles at him! He was going thru the trail to the grocery store, and they started throwing things at him! He was holding a place on his head and showing mama his hand. I learned that he had a nub thumb. One of the bottles had cut him on the back of his head, and the other had cut him on his already, chopped off finger! Man, kids can be so cruel! Mama brought him inside the house and got him cleaned up and put some ointment that she used for us when we got hurt. We knew what that meant! We were all hovering around him, smiling and letting him know he was in good hands. He ate like he had never eaten before! We kept putting food on his plate. He smiled the whole time. I felt an immediate bond with this man. It's almost as if he came to my window, on the day that I came home to visit, so….it must mean that I should look out for him. I never considered that I was too young to look out for grownups. I just always believed that God wanted me to look out for the underdog.

I remember one morning, Mama, Nadine, and their friend Dave were sitting in the kitchen, having coffee and beer. Yes, beer. At least Dave came over with a beer in his hand. We had already had our breakfast, and were on to watching cartoons, and some of us were coloring in our coloring books. I always had one ear and eye on what I was doing, and one on my surroundings. Mama, always read the newspaper as she had her coffee each morning. Nadine came over to wash clothes. Dave apparently was having a very bad morning. He looked and smelled like he had been up all night. Mama could tell you everything that was going on around her as she read the newspaper. I couldn't figure out how she did that! The paper was always raised up high enough to cover her whole head. But, she would calmly say to whoever was doing something they shouldn't, to stop doing what they were doing. Well, Dave was murmuring about all of his woes in life, and Nadine wasn't trying to hear it. "Dave, don't come over here this morning with all that crying and shit! It's too damned early in the morning to be dranking and crying anyway!" she yelled at him. The words she said to him pierced me to my heart. For one, mama wasn't paying much attention to him, and Nadine was cussing him out! I felt so sorry for him. I just kept my head down to my paper and coloring, but, I just told Dave, "Jesus love you Dave, and he will be your friend when nobody else will." Dave looked at me, and a hush came over the whole room. He started crying for real then! I thought I had said something to hurt him. Mama, not lowering her paper at all, explained to me that those were tears of joy he was crying. I just got up and went to him and gave him a big hug. It was like he was a little child that didn't have any cry left in him. He just collapsed over my shoulders, and sighed like the weight of the world had been lifted off of his shoulders! I remember patting him on his back like he was my little boy, and wiping the tears off of his face with the napkin from the table. Nadine just sashayed by and told me to go sit down somewhere. Mama had to put her in check then. "Look Nadine, you need to realize when God is moving and learn to shut your mouth sometimes!" She walled her eyes at mama and me, and went down the hall with her coffee. Dave, looked like he had gotten a new life, and get this….he sobered up right before our eyes!

Well, mama marched right over to the church to find out who did all of this to Dummy. She gave them a piece of her mind, and told them they were the very ones that made other people in the neighborhood not want to come to that church. She told the kids as well as the adults. She then made it perfectly clear that the law would be coming to deal with what they had done to Dummy, and God was gonna deal with their souls!

We fed Dummy, and sat him on the couch, and before you know it…he was sound asleep. I watched him for a long time. Thoughts of why God let him be like that? Why he had to get his thumb cut off? Why were the kids so mean to him? All these things ran thru my mind as I sat there and watched him sleep. Mama, stayed fired up all evening behind that. When the police finally came…mama had to tell them about themselves for taking so long. She figured because it was just Dummy…they didn't feel it was important enough to hurry. She gave them hell!

They tried to give mama this spill about Dummy raping a girl in the hood. Mama, made it clear that any news in the hood came straight to her door, she didn't have to seek it out. If he had raped anyone...she and everybody else would have known. She opened the door for the two officers, and told them, "Take that lie to some fool that believes y'all." They dropped their heads and hurried out of Jazzy's house.

You know, the Lord has a way of preparing us for things that are ahead. All of the time that Dummy was coming around us, taking out the trash, playing marbles with Malcolm, with his good thumb. All of the times he would have to gesture and sign to us what he wanted us to know. Each and every one of those things, were helping to prepare us for, little did we know, was going to be one of the most major turn arounds in our lives in the Projects. Little did we know that the things that Dummy brought to our lives was gonna help us to relate to...oops! I'm getting a little ahead of myself.

By and by, Dummy would begin to come around to my tree. Eventually; he climbed up in the tree to cautiously get a feel of whether I would let him come up any further to hang out, and keep me company in my tree. I would not even let my brother in that tree! Dummy became a child all over again as he climb up there with me! He just grinned and grinned. I didn't have to worry about him talking too much if I was trying to think. I believe he knew when I was in that state of mind. He would just sit there and eat whatever we brought up, and watched all the comings and goings of the hood. I felt like it was somehow my duty to befriend him. He pointed out the kids that did all the mean things to him from the tree to me. I ran it down to my brother and cousins. Between playing football, wrestling, and tripping the girls up playing jump rope or jumping board...we got each and every one of them back for Dummy! They just conveniently got hurt playing somehow? Dummy would just hang on the side line, sitting on the side walk like a little kid, watching us do our magic to get them back. He would crack up when we let him know on the low that that was for him. He just became a fixture in our family. We didn't think it strange, because mama always took in a stray dog, or someone that was down on their luck. That's how we meet JoJo, and L.B. They were shunned by some of the other families in the hood, but mama, took them right under her wings. She showed them how to carry themselves without making them feel judged.

As the week came to a close, I knew it would be time for me to go back to the Tyler's house. I was kinda sad, yet glad that I had the best of both worlds. My big sister Miriam had the awful chore of having to shampoo my hair. She hated it! I was such a tomboy I got grass and tons of dirt in my hair playing with the boys. I would get a whipping every day for it! I would still ease back out and do the exact same thing the next day. Mama was a stay at home mom for a while. Her other sisters would go out and work. She had to cook, wash clothes and see to 11 kids every day during the summer, and help to get us off to school thru the whole year of school! On the weekends, she got with Nadine, and let her hair hang low! I should say her wigs hang low. She had a wig for every occasion, and every style you could imagine! I didn't understand why she wore them, she had beautiful hair!

Miriam would fuss the whole time she was doing me and Sasha's hair! We had to hang over the bathroom sink, while we stood on the toilet seat. Misery! I almost always found a way to slip and fall. She would pound me flat up the middle of my bare back with her open palm to deal with me. I think I hated her at those times, as much as she hated us when it was time to do our hair. We had a lot of hair to deal with too. Times were good then. You could let your daughters run and play outside with no shirt on when they were smaller kids. After we got our hair shampooed, we would run out in our shorts to play so it could air dry. I think we did it to get out of mama, and Miriam's way, until they cooled down from the mess we made in the bathroom, and mama having to cuss Miriam out for being so mean to us.

I saw Dummy coming down the sidewalk, so, I ran in the house to put on my shirt, and shoes so we could get up in the Crepe. Sasha was a bit envious of our friendship, because I would drop what I was doing with her to go up the tree to hang with him. I had to let her know that I had to explain to him that I had to get ready to go over to the Tyler's and would be gone for a while. That started up another issue. She wanted to know why I was so special that I could go live with my teacher and none of them were able to go. I told her maybe her teacher didn't like her the way mine liked me. You do know that was fighting material, right? Me, and Sasha didn't need much for us to throw blows. We got a whipping for breakfast, lunch, dinner, and a sleeping pill whipping! It still didn't stop us from having at least two brawls a day for something! Almost anything would do to trigger a fight. Guess who had to break the fight up? That's right, Dummy. He was so upset to see us fighting, he was crying! It broke my heart to hear him cry. It was a pitiful, mourning sound because of his deafness. Jazzy had to whip us for fighting, and for making Dummy cry! What kind of madness is that?! I took that one in stride though, because I had hurt Dummy, and I knew I would be leaving soon. They didn't get whippings at the Tyler's.

When I dried up from my whipping, and Dummy dried up from seeing us fighting, and getting a whipping…we grabbed some cookies, and headed for the tree. Ya know what? I don't even think Dummy would come up the tree with me, if I didn't feed him. That was his favorite pass time, to come over our house, because he knew he would be fed. When I found an easy way to tell him I was leaving for a while, he started crying again! Then, I had to bribe him by telling him he needed to get in my tree for me every day about this time so he could watch it for me. He was so proud to do that for me. I guess he felt that he was important, if I would let him, and, him only get in my tree while I was away. I told mama about it, and she just hugged me and told me how much I thought just like she did. She laughed at the thought she had in that moment. "What you laughing 'bout mama?" "What are you laughing about Mama?" She corrected my grammar. She was a very articulate woman when she had to be. When she hung out with her buddies…all kinds of slang came out of her mouth! She told me she was laughing at the thought of her having to whip Dummy if some of my ways rubbed off on him from hanging up in that Crepe Myrtle too much! We laughed a while as we imagined what that would be like. I was gonna miss my mama every day that I was away. It didn't make a difference how many times a day I got my butt whipped…after all was said and done, I knew she did it because she wanted a better and a right way for her children. She made us to realize, because you lived in the hood…you didn't have to let the mentality of the hood live in you! Some of the people called her stuck up. She didn't even care. Those were the kind of people she was trying to teach us to avoid the mind set of. They knew one thing for certain though…they better not bother her kid's! They had heard how she whipped men down that tried to clown her! She was classy when she needed to be, spiritual, all the time, and could get down and dirty with best of 'em, if she had to. Jazzy, knew who she was, and didn't give a damn who thought contrary to who she was! She loved who would let her love them, she prayed for ignorant people, and she was gonna tell you something about the Lord before you left her presence!

That's just what she did too before I left for the Tyler's. She encouraged me to pray often, treat the boys like I wanted to be treated, and give God thanks for letting me be a part of such nice things, and the kindness the Tylers showed me while I was there with them.

Chapter 4

A Sad Day at the Tyler's

Well, the part of treating the boys the way I wanted to be treated was tested soon as I got there! Just as you figured, everyone greeted me with open arms…except Jeremy. He acted as if he could care less that I was back! Why did he always act this way with me? I had had many fights with my partners and enemies in the hood since the fight we had by the bathroom! We all made up and were playing football and stuff like it didn't even matter. Jeremy, on the other hand was still holding something against me! Robby, was my one saving grace. If he wasn't being a good brother, I don't know how I would get thru the rest of the summer! If I tried to watch anything funny on TV with them…I didn't dare laugh at anything funny. Jeremy would roll his eyes at me and tell me that it wasn't funny. He would deliberately not laugh, so I wouldn't. Robby had had enough! I saw a side of him I hadn't seen. He reached over the table and grabbed Jeremy by the collar, got around that table so fast Jeremy didn't know what was going on! Robby held him pent up against the wall so tight, he couldn't move! He told him if he treated me mean one more time in his presence…he was gonna make him regret the day he was born! Then, he said something that made my jaw drop! "If, you like her the way you say you do, you got a funny way of showing it!" In walked Mr. Tyler. He wanted to know what Robby had just said, not why he had Jeremy up against the wall. I was still sitting there with my mouth wide open! Mrs. Tyler dropped me off and went to the fabric shop. I was scared, because I had heard Mr. Tyler jump in Jeremy's behind before! I didn't know who was gonna get it this time?? I got up and went to my room, and got in the closet! It wasn't my tree, but it would have to do for now. I didn't want to see him hurt Robby, because he was so sweet. Nor, did I want him to hurt my future husband, which it turned out, really did like me! I don't know which emotion was the strongest…my fear, or my fantasy?? I heard a lot of commotion in the front. I heard Robby yell, "Stop lying Jeremy! You know you said you like her more than for a sister! Tell the truth!" Mr. Tyler began to go down the list of the many times he had told Jeremy his intentions concerning him and I. Jeremy, it sounded like, tried to push past Mr. T., big mistake. "Who the Hell you think you pushing past boy? I see the problem. Oh yeah, I see the problem. You ain't had yo ass whipped in a good while. I'm gone fix that right now!" The next thing I heard was the swoosh, and the connection of Mr. T's belt against Jeremy's body! I was agonizing in my soul for him! I had to cover my ears in the closet to keep from hearing all of the many times he struck him. Robby ran past my room, and shut the door to his room to keep from watching, and hearing Jeremy's cry.

That was the saddest day I had experienced in a long time. When Jeremy was finally turned loose…his sobs could be heard outside of his room. Mr. T, got his keys, got in his truck, and left. I felt so much hate for him, and now Robby. I knew Robby was trying to defend me. But, I would have rather not known how Jeremy felt about me, and continued in misery with the way he was treating me; than to have this happen to Jeremy. I cried, because he was crying.

Robby, eased into my room. When he didn't see me, he knew to look in the closet, because, I had confided in him about my tree. He had tears in his eyes. He just squatted down and told me he didn't mean for it to happen that way, over and over. The more he said it, the more I cried. He just sat there with me. After I calmed down a bit, I asked him did Jeremy really like me. He told me that that was the reason he acted so crazy towards me! I was totally confused! He had to show me how boys show their likes different from girls.

At that moment, I jumped up to go see about Jeremy. Robby, tried to grab my arm, and warned me that Jeremy may not want me to come in there. I kept past him. I didn't knock. I walked right up to him, as he laid his head on his desk still sobbing inwardly. He didn't raise his head as I put my arm across his back, and pat him softly, and told him in his ear, "I'm sorry I got you hurt Jeremy. It's gonna be alright. Please, don't cry no more." He raised his head up, looked at me, nostrils flaring, breathing hard, and told me, "I hate you!" If, Robby hadn't told me about the boy way/girl way thing, I think I would've have been devastated! I just looked at him with compassion, and nodded as if I understood, lean over and kissed him on his cheek, and walked out. You know what let me know he didn't mean those words he said? That's right. He didn't try to strike me, or resist me kissing him! I was ok then. I think he was too. We didn't hear him sobbing anymore, and, he came out of his room, and went to Robby's room, and sat there on the bed quietly. I feel it was his way of letting him know that he was no longer mad at him. I secretly thought that he wanted to thank him because the truth was out, and he got, not only a hug of comfort, but, a kiss too! I eased back to my room, and stayed in my rocker until Mrs. Tyler came and woke me up. Then I got scared. She wanted to know what happened while she was away. I told her, I was in my room, in the closet, and I didn't know. Of course, that led to…"Why was I in the closet?" I told her that that was where I went when I was afraid. She looked at me, patted me on my leg, and left the room. I guess she couldn't deal with that at the time. I sure wasn't gonna give her anything to work with to get Jeremy in more trouble with her!

If ever you want to bring all of the dignity out of a very prim and proper woman…just abuse one of her kids in some way! By the time Robby told the whole story to Mrs. T., and, she saw the whelts on Jeremy's back and arms…the house sounded like a war zone! I thought Nadine could cuss! Nadine didn't have a thing on this 1st grade, classy, school teacher! She yelled out threats of what she would do to her husband if he even thought about putting his hands on either one of her boys again! She threw stuff at him, and talked about his mammy too! I was beyond shocked! I was hurt for Mr. T. though. He couldn't get a word in to explain, and it seemed like the whole family was on Mrs. T.'s side. I was happy that she got onto him about the way he did Jeremy. That was very mean how he whipped him without even allowing him a chance to say his heart about the whole thing.

I was ready to go home at that point. I felt like things were probably fine at their house, that is; until I came. At breakfast the next morning it was very quiet and awkward to everyone. Jeremy didn't raise his eyes to look at anyone at the table. Robby, struggled to figure out how to ***be***, without being funny or super nice to everyone. All that you could hear was the spoons and forks clinking against the plates and bowls. Mrs. Tyler still had an edge on everything she said to anyone. Mr. T. just ate as fast as he could and left the table to go off to the woods to work. Jeremy wasn't allowed to go with him that morning, per Mrs. T's orders. Just think; all of this time, I thought Mr. T. was running things! There's just something about the fury of a woman about her kids. You can do nothing to appease her, but stay the hell out of the way of her and her little ones! I didn't know how I was gonna make Mr. T. ever like me being there again. I was afraid if I told mama the real reason for wanting to come home, she wouldn't let me go back over there. Then, I really wouldn't be able to grow up with my future husband! I sure wished I could get to my tree so I could think of a solution, and pray for this family to be back to normal. I went to MY ROOM, and sat back in the rocking chair, and brushed my grandma's hair on the rag doll she made me. It made me feel the closest connection to the tree as possible when I did that. Then, I had an idea. I waited until Mrs. T. went into the sewing room to work on her things like she did on Saturdays. I eased in her room to use the phone, and called to speak to my grandmother.

My nosy cousin, Deginna answered the phone. She had to give me the third degree about what I wanted to talk to my grandma about? After much word maneuvering (well; lying) she got her to the phone. By the time I explained everything that happened, and what led up to it. I made her promise me she wouldn't tell Jazzy about me having a crush on Jeremy.

My grandma was not at all surprised. She told me that kids have hearts just like grown- ups. They feel love, and they feel hurt too. I asked her why Nadine, called it being "Fast Tailed" then? She said, "Nadine been hot all of her life. So that's what she think is on everybody else's mind." We laughed, and I felt better. She did let me know that I was not supposed to let no boy even think about putting their hands in my "Spot" as she called it! I assured her that I didn't like him in that way. I asked her to let this be our secret, and she reminded me that she had never told the others, so why would she start now. I loved my grandma. She was very understanding! She always had a way of putting things into perspective. I hung up the phone, and had a glow in my heart. I knew I could get thru the rest of the summer at the Tyler's.

I wasn't quite sure at first, why Mr. T was being overly nice. But, the whole day he did all kinds of things that were not unusual, but…a little bit much. For a man that was as reserved as he was; he normally did what he did with barely a word unless it was necessary. He was cracking jokes with me and the boys, offering us snacks that we are not allowed to have before dinner, and anything was Go! We would all sneak peeks out of the corner of our eyes at each other to see if it was just us, or was it him? Mrs. Tyler, tried to play hard for a few days, but, she couldn't stay out of her element forever. She even tried to laugh at a few of the corny jokes Mr. T. was trying to tell. I was glad because I felt sorry for him. He had tried to show Jeremy over and over again, how sorry he was. He just did it without words of "I'm sorry for beating you so bad."

Jeremy spent each day in his own little space, away from everybody unless it was necessary to be around us. He would go out of the way all the more to avoid me now. Even though Mr. T. was being all extra, he still was trying to keep the enemy close. If he got us all together as much as he could; he wouldn't have to worry about what was going on when we were out of his sight. I noticed, if I was in the room, and Jeremy was not….Mr. T. didn't have to try as hard. He had me where he could see me. Mrs. T. tried to get me interested in her sewing room, and all that was a part of that. I admit, she had much nicer stuff than my mom. But, mama did more creative work than she did. I learned how to make pillow covers and embroider little flowers on the ends of them. I was really proud of that. I still had rather be in the other room with the boys wrestling and seeing the smile on Mr. Tyler's face. It really mattered to me that he was not hurting any more. I believe it would have been over long before now if, he had just SAID he was sorry. Then again, maybe he wasn't sorry.

Chapter 5

KeAna Gets Some Balls!

I began to wonder, for some strange reason, about my old friend Pamela. She used to be cool. Pamela was my tomboy buddy. We got into all of the mischief we could think of at the Baptist Kindergarten that I attended! Mrs. Newton, would have us line up to go into the chapel for Devotion each morning. Single file, left hand on the shoulder of the person in front of you, NO TALKING! Me, and Pamela could hardly wait to get to the Chapel. We knew that Mrs. Newton's piano playing was going to overshadow our lil schemes to scare all of the prissy girls in the pews. We would chew up Sugar Babies, (that's a candy we bought at the candy lady) because they were soft and chewy, dark caramel….and crawl under the pews to the feet of the stuck up girls. While, Mrs. Newton banged "Yes, Jesus loves me" on the piano; me and Pamela would lay out in the floor, flat on our backs, gagging like we were choking to death, and saying our tonsils were coming up out of us! They squalled and kicked and bought it every time! We knew we would get in trouble and have to sit by ourselves to be gazing stocks in front of the rest of the class. The upset that we gave to the "Goody two shoesers" was well worth it to us. There was one girl in the class that was as skinny as a rail! She had the prettiest clothes, and long pony tails. I didn't know it at the time. But, the aroma, I thought, that smelt like Chicken Noodle soup that she had about her…., I learned later on in life that it was the need for her to use a deodorant! I didn't know a kindergartener needed to wear Deodorant! But, she did. I always liked hanging with her more. Pamela didn't like it one bit! I felt she was controlling and jealous anyway. After spending time with KeAna, I realized it was time to stop hanging with the likes of Pamela. When I was with KeAna, there was no gossip, or talking bad about other girls, or bullying going on like it was with Pamela. I liked the new change.

Pamela became green with envy about me being with KeAna each day! So much so, she started spitting out threats about beating up KeAna at lunchtime. She knew not to threaten me. I had already had to let her know about messing with me during the summer in front of her house! She would whisper ugly things about KeAna being a "Bag of Bones", and other things that hurt her feelings. I had to school her about how to handle Pamela. KeAna's mom was a Teacher at the Jr. High School. KeAna was well mannered, didn't know a thing about the slang of the hood, much less about how to get someone up off of you. I told her she needed to come over and play football with me and the boys if she wanted to toughen up enough to be ready for Pamela. That didn't go too well. She was so frail; the first time she played, as soon as they pounced on her…she cried like a baby! I had to tell the guys to go light on her. Guess what? The same thing that my brother told me about crying when I played, worked for her! When I told her that her crying was gonna make them not want to let her play. She soon learned to take a slamming pretty well. I was able to talk to Pamela, to keep her off of KeAna for a while. But, the day came when she made sure the whole school knew she was full to the top with everybody bragging on KeAna.

There was a mound of dirt in the far corner of the field of the playground. It was there to be spread over the field for a future, softball field. Well, KeAna had gotten a pair of balls about herself! She let it be known that, the hill of dirt was gonna be Pamela's burial ground. She was gonna knock Pamela, clean to the other side of the hill on her butt! Whoa! That's what I was trying to get her to thinking like. I had to show her how standing up to a bully was ok. They don't know what you have in your artillery anyway. Well; I found out that I had created a beast! The day came when Pamela, named the time and the place. KeAna came to school with her hair braided flat to her head, in two big braids. When I saw it, I laughed at her. She explained that it was done that way because, Pamela was not about to pull her hair! Her theory was, Pamela wasn't even gonna get one blow in! She had prepared to knock Pamela, clean across the dirt hill before she even knew what hit her! You know what? That's exactly what happened! Everybody gathered to go out to the field. KeAna took off running full speed! Those skinny legs of hers were flying! Everyone thought she was running scared. Not so. She made it to the top of the hill, stood there with her hands on her boney hips, and waited for everyone to get there. Pamela got there, eyeballed KeAna, and proceeded with hesitation up the hill. I believe she had second thoughts. I guess she didn't believe KeAna would call her bluff. Just when she got arm's length, or should I say, a fist's length away from KeAna; all we saw was KeAna's fist connect with Pamela's head! Pamela went rolling down the other side of the hill, and KeAna was down on her with lightning speed! Bam, bop, wop, all upside of Pamela's head! I felt sorry for Pamela, a little bit anyway. The crowd was going crazy! Me, and my brother, Malcolm, had to pull KeAna off of Pamela! Pamela rolled up in a ball and tried to cover her head. KeAna had to do one more thing before she was finished with her. She bent down, got a handful of dirt, and threw it in Pamela's face! Boyyyy, we laughed, and Malcolm took KeAna's lil arm, stuck it in the air, and everybody began to chant, "Ali, Ali, Ali!" KeAna was grinning from ear, to ear. I was so proud of her! I really began to feel sorry for Pamela when, everybody left her out in the field by herself. It served her right though. She had spent so much time, bullying kids that were (what she thought)…weaker than her. Mrs. Tyler was very upset with both KeAna and me. She told us that we should have told her what had been going on, all along. I knew if we did that, KeAna would never get to prove she was not a weakling. Mrs. Tyler gave us this line about not using violence, as this black Civil Rights Activist and Preacher named Dr. Martin Luther King Jr. was telling everyone at that time.

While growing up in the hood, violence was the only way we were taught to get results when we were backed into a corner. Mama always taught us though, "Because you have to live in "The Hood" for now…you don't have to act like "The Hood", ***ever***!" Well; we did that day! KeAna thought she would be in big trouble at home, so she asked me if I could walk her home to help her explain to her mom how Pamela had been picking on her, and the reason why she had started playing football with me and the boys from the beginning. When her mom heard our story and the one from the Principal…she was elated that KeAna had finally gotten some balls too! She called my mother to tell her where I was, and to thank her for letting me be a friend to KeAna. She never had any real friends, except the ones on her street. This became one truly genuine relationship. She was either at my house, or, I was at hers..

Chapter 6

That Military Guy

Remember Dummy? Remember how I said that, "Things happen in your life to prepare you for your future."? Well, we weren't prepared for this one! We thought. My mom had practically raised us without a man being there for her full time. Her husband was a military guy. He had many tours that kept him away for long periods at a time. I guess the strain of it all took a toll on the relationship they had. I saw him 1 time that I remembered. That time, I shall never forget. He came home when I was almost 7. Mama was down the hall in her bedroom. Her sisters had moved out. Each of them got their own apartment. This left things very quiet at our house! Me, Miriam, and Sasha were in the front playing around in front of the television. Malcolm was out playing marbles in the backyard. We didn't hear a knock at the door. I remember Miriam leaping up from the floor with joy! I saw this sailor towering over us, scooping up Miriam, then, reaching down to pick up Sasha in the other arm. He reached over me to get Sasha. He headed down the hall. I ran up behind him to pat him on his leg to get him to pick me up too. He shifted Sasha into the arm he was holding Miriam in, reached back with his free arm, pushed me back from him like I was pestering him! I knew that day that this man couldn't be my dad! I stopped in my tracks and froze! The trembling on the inside that drove me to my tree ran deep at that moment. I couldn't even run to my tree! All I could do was, stand there and watch him walk down, what seemed like a very long hall! "Why didn't he pick me up?" "Why didn't he even speak to me, or pat me on the head like the family dog or something?!" That was the first scar of rejection that I had experienced apart from Jeremy. But, to experience it from the man I was told was my daddy! That hurt so bad! I was sick in my stomach. I could hear mama, and, nem in the room laughing and hugging and bragging on how good one to the other looked, and kisses being placed on Miriam and Sasha's cheeks. I tried to remove myself from that spot to run to my tree. I just couldn't move! I didn't know how much that day would affect me. But, it did. In ways I never thought it would. Even though he was away a lot, the affect was not so bad because we had a lot of love there among ourselves. There was adventure, and sharing. If Ms. Rosie knew your mom good....she would let you have cookies and snacks from her corner store. If you needed something to cook...Mr. Sam gave you credit at his meat market until the 1st of the month. The mothers in the hood always passed around clothing that was too little for one child, to the family that had less in the hood. But, there was never a time in my days there that I was ever treated like this man had just treated me. I always felt safe there. Today was different. It was cold, even though outside, it was a beautiful, sunny day. It was a feeling of dread, and gloom that I hadn't experienced before. You know the really sad thing about it? Jazzy never came out of the room to call me in, nor Malcolm to be a part of this reunion. Malcolm was just outside of the back door. I was still there in that spot, frozen and feeling like my best friend had died.

That evening, me and Malcolm were conveniently picked up by Nadine to go over to her house for the weekend. Even as a 6 year old, I knew it had something to do with that man in the uniform being at our house. Nadine was trying to go out of her way to be all extra towards us. She bought me a new doll, and a bow and arrow set for Malcolm. It still didn't help that feeling to ebb out of my chest any more than, the moment it was first put there. Nadine's son Tommy always knew how to put a smile on my face, or to bring me to tears. He could tell as soon as he saw me that I was on the verge of tears. He coaxed me off to the play house we had made up of an old, abandoned house next door to their house. "Are you ready to tell me why you look like that and ain't running yo big mouth today? I tried to laugh at him, but nothing came out but a big sob, and tears I didn't even know I had in me! He was helpless to get anything out of me, but that. Then he took out running when I had cried so much, I started throwing up, what looked like my guts! He ran and got Nadine. She came, wiped my face with the cold towel she brought with her, sat down on the floor of that old house, and pulled me to her lap, and just rocked me until I stopped shaking. She didn't ask me why I was crying because she already knew.

Malcolm had a way of "blocking", as they called it. He was never around to hold my hand. He was always gone. It's like he could tell when the bad stuff was coming. He would always be around the corner or down the block somewhere. He didn't like to hang around the house when Jazzy had her friends over for the weekend. He only came in on the session where they had gotten full of booze, and started giving us money to dance for them. He knew how to dance, and he wanted to get all the money he could to go to the candy lady in the hood! Our cousin Raymond could out dance us all though! He was short, pigeon toed, and bow legged! James Brown, "The King of Soul" as he was called in those days only *thought* he was dancing! Raymond could do the splits, the Camel Walk, and everything James Brown did...only better! Malcolm didn't care. He just wanted in on the money. Then, you didn't see him anymore that evening until the street lights came on.

Even when Tommy told him I was crying my heart out, he stayed out in the yard, just rolling the old tire off of somebody's car, up and down the dirt road they lived on. I think that he was trying to protect himself somehow from hurt. I can honestly say…I've never seen him cry!

I wondered why Tommy always hung so close to me. He would even sing to me when I got a whipping. He would sit on the floor beside the bed, or the couch and sing…."Oh My Darling" to me until I would cry myself to sleep. I didn't know it at that time, but, I would learn later why he did these things. Ella was Nadine's oldest daughter. She was always trying to be the regulator when we played. She ***had*** to be the Mama, the Teacher, and the Sunday school Teacher when we played Church! She had to be the boss of everything! I recall getting the worse whipping I had ever gotten from Nadine. Listening to Ella, I let her talk me into walking this cute lil boy home, and; holding his hand, as we walked down the dirt road together. Who comes around the corner from the grocery store? That's right. Nadine and her new boyfriend! He was the one that spotted us trying to run thru the trail so we wouldn't get caught. I didn't even have sense enough to let his hand go free as we ran! This new boyfriend of hers was already getting on our nerves. Now, he had the nerve to rat us out to Nadine! We would've made it if he had kept his fat, black mouth shut! Nadine did it so smooth like…..it made me hate her! She made us put up all the groceries, then…she sent us to the switch bush to get, not one, but, four switches! Man, she whipped us until we couldn't even cry no more! We were just dry crying! I was dancing in circles the whole time she was whipping me, then, I danced out the room spinning in circles even after she let me loose! I wanted mama to come and get me NOW!! I was wondering why Tommy wasn't there trying to comfort me! Neither Tommy, nor Malcolm would come inside. I know they heard us screaming to the top of our lungs! To make matters worse; Ella had the nerve to act like it was my fault we got in trouble! It was her bossiness that made me hold Jasper's hand in the first place! She rolled her pop eyes at me all evening! I did my usual; I retreated to the old play house since I couldn't go to my tree. I could hardly wait for mama to come get me! I thought so anyway. How come when she got there….I got another whipping! It wasn't bad enough that she had put me away from their "Happy Family" moment with the military guy. It was like pouring gasoline in my wounds, and striking a match to my heart again! All of this pain in the run of one day! I wished that I could go to the Tyler's. Then, I thought about how Jeremy had treated me the last time I was there. I didn't have anywhere to go from the madness! I wanted my tree!!!

Sunday school, I realized was where I found comfort, apart from my tree. There was always a lesson that spoke to the very place I was at that time in my life. Who would've thunk it! Ms. Newton was speaking about Joseph being sold out by his brothers! That's exactly how I felt! Mama had sold me out for that military person, Ella put me on the block for Jasper, and Nadine let the word of a man, she had just met mind you; cause her to beat me tearless! I felt so forsaken. Then, right there, the next morning in church, I was comforted by the story of a boy that did nothing to his brothers at all. Yet, he was left to possibly die in the wild by his older brothers. The end of the story was what gave me the bubbly feeling in my stomach and chest. I didn't understand at that time, that was, what I learned was the "Joy of the Lord" in my spirit taking place! It was beautifully strong, yet calming and brought such a peace to me! I still had all the scars of my whipping the day before all over me. But, the feeling on the inside made me forget all about the scars in my heart as well.

Chapter 7

"Lord, where's Dummy?"

I knew that morning when I woke up it was gonna be a crazy day. I didn't wet the bed, and, I fell out of the bed! That's what woke me up! I was in the room alone. That certainly was weird. I usually had to crawl over Sasha, and Sharletta to get out. It was a crazy quiet in the house! I gathered myself from the floor, went to pee a river because, my bladder was full from not wetting the bed. When I came to the front of the house, no one was in the living room, or the kitchen. I went out the door to see where everyone was. Several people were gathered in different circles. Some with their heads dropped not saying anything. Some were crying that silent cry we cry when we are too heavy inside to let it out without losing it. That's the look I saw on mama's face. I ran to her to see what the matter was. When she saw me, it got worse. Everyone was looking at me like they all were keeping some great secret from me. I looked at them, then to mama. No one said a word! I began to pull mama by the hand away from everyone. I felt I needed to ask her in secret what was going on. She sat me down on the stoop and put her hand, gently on my face. I knew then, it had something to do with me, and would hurt me. I just started shaking my head. That helped me to block out what she was about to say. She put both of her hands on my face then. I could see around her that everyone was watching us. In my mind, I made myself to look straight past them into NO WHERE. Whatever it was….I just didn't want to know. I had just had enough the weekend before. I came home from Nadine's to get to my tree, and to hang out with Dummy because, he would just let me sulk all I wanted to and eat his snacks quietly. Well, he was nowhere to be found. Jazzy had to take him to the emergency room in a taxi. The low down people that had cars on the block wouldn't even let him in their car! Then, they wonder why they were living in poverty all of their days. When Jazzy got him to the hospital, they acted like he was too dirty for them to examine him! You already know that Jazzy got crunk to the max! She made it clear that she would wash Dummy's black ass herself if she had to! But, he wasn't leaving there until someone checked him out and found out what was causing him to have the high fever he kept having! Well, as it turned out; they had to keep Dummy there! Somehow the nubbed thumb had gotten infected.

We always waited for Jazzy to return from the hospital to tell us how Dummy was doing. All week long, she was acting grouchy with us after leaving the hospital. She would fuss about the one or two dishes in the sink, or a toy being on the floor out of place. But, she never said much about Dummy. Today, she had to tell me how Dummy was doing. I was sitting there with my walls up, all around me. I continued to stare across the heads of the people behind Jazzy. She was calling my name, but, I refused to hear what I already knew she was going to tell me. I just stared ahead and I felt the tears start to roll down my face, under my neck, and into my lap. I just sat there, shaking and crying, as Jazzy tried to make me understand that Dummy's fever wouldn't go away, and his thumb was too infected by the time he went to the hospital for him to get better in time. All I could do was sit there and cry silently and wonder who was gonna sit with me in my tree, and keep me company, and be my trusted friend. Dummy was the one friend that looked up to me, and he looked to me for food, and protection. He was the one that I could count on to be there when I came from the Tyler's or Nadine's nem house. Jazzy had always told me that Jesus was a healer for the sick. Why didn't he heal Dummy? Did he feel that Dummy was not worth it like all of the other folk in the hood felt? I was mad at Jazzy, I was mad at all of the people in the hood, but, I was mad the most at God! He could heal Dummy, and he didn't! I couldn't understand that one. My little mind was full of questions at that moment. I moved mama's hands from me, stood up, and yelled to all of the people standing around. "What y'all standing around crying for? None of y'all even loved Dummy! None of y'all ever treated him nice!" I ran around the corner to my tree, and climbed it with lightning speed, and sat up there and cried myself sick! It was my grandmother that talked me down from the tree. She convinced me that I was not doing Dummy no good by acting that way. She showed me the many times that Dummy had wanted people to be at peace with each other, and not act angry at each other. I remembered that as well, and came down. I still wanted to be mad at God though. He let Dummy die, and he could've stopped it from happening!

They had Dummy's funeral at a Funeral Parlor. The church in the neighborhood wouldn't even let him have his funeral there! They said he wasn't a member there! I didn't want to go back there ever again! When mama made us go, for a long time, I would just sit at the back and roll my eyes at the preacher, and the ushers really made me mad! They tried to act all nice and helpful to the people when they came in. The only thing I could remember is, some of their very children had been the ones that threw rocks at Dummy!

There was an old lady on the block that we lived in named Ms. Holly. That's what we called her anyway. She would always cook up the best Tea cakes in the world, and give them to mama and nem. I would run over to her house when I couldn't get my way at Jazzy's. She really relished in this. She would fix me up a plate of biscuits and gravy and whatever meat she had prepared. Those were the best biscuits! Whew! She could always tell when I was sad about something. I guess everybody was talking about how hard I had taken Dummy's death. I was right, because, as soon as I finished eating, she told me to come and sit with her on the studio sofa cot. That's what the old people called it in the south. When I did, she asked me was I still mad at everybody about Dummy. I told her I only had a problem with God about it. She didn't even act like she was surprised at all! She began to remind me of all the times Dummy had been mistreated. I just nodded in agreement. Then she showed me how God gets to a point where he makes people leave you alone. I explained to her that no one was being mean to Dummy anymore since he had been hanging with me in my tree. She then began to tell me the stories she had heard about them not wanting to touch him at the hospital, because they felt he had germs, and was dirty all of the time. That didn't help at all! I started a new hatred for the hospital people!

I made it make sense for me that, God was taking Dummy to heaven, because, he didn't want anybody else mistreating him. The people at the hospital, well, they were the last straw! They took a vow to be kind and help the sick! Instead, they treated Dummy like he was a no-count, and basically let him die from neglecting him! I was very angry, and for a long time. I think that's what made things so hard on Delores, Miriam's best friend.

Chapter 8

"It's My Party Nadine!"

Mama got this brilliant idea, from somewhere! Why, I will never know. It sure wasn't something I was in favor of. She decided to have a double birthday party for me, and Delores! Delores ate you out of house and home if you invited her to any type of food eating event! She was a chunky ole thang! She didn't care who she begged food of, as long as it was edible! Me, and Dummy always took our snacks up the Crepe Myrtle to keep her from mooching off of us when she came over to see Miriam. Dummy couldn't talk. But, I bet ya bottom dollar, if he could….he would cuss Delores' big butt out for begging so much!!

Now, here it is my 8th birthday; and Jazzy wants me to share my jar of money that she had been saving for me all summer long, and have a birthday cake made for the two of us to share! Boy was I pissed! Why did she, of all people have to have the same birthday as I did? She was already trying to steal my big sister from me! Now, to have to share my money, my cake and ice cream too! I cried, and had temper tantrums the whole week leading up to the party. To top it off; I got my tail beat the day of the party for acting such a fool about it all!

I was about sick and tired of Nadine! She was determined to make this party about HER! Her and L.B. had smoked enough of that loud smelling cigarette stuff, so much that you could smell them before they even came around the corner! This just pumped her head up all the more. She kept coming in the kitchen sneaking food for her and L.B.! Big Mama, (that's what we called our grandma) told Jazzy, "You need to come get Nadine and all of her drunkardness up out of my kitchen! They need to stop smoking that shit! She already keeps up enough mess as it is." I was so glad to hear her get in trouble for a change. She stayed over our house some weekends and she kept us laughing or crying! She tried to steal the spot light, by talking about the birthday outfit that Mrs. Tyler had bought me. I rather liked my little yellow shorts and red patent leather sandals. I just didn't like the feeling the elastic tube top that was a part of the outfit. It made me feel all itchy! But, I was feeling pretty and I felt the need to walk and show off my new stuff. The new boy down the sidewalk hadn't seen me dressed up. He only saw me looking tattered and torn from playing football with Malcolm nem. I just knew I had to get Nadine out of my hair! I figured out a way to ease through the crowd of the uninvited, saw an opportunity, and took it!

I put on my little red sunglasses that matched my sandals. I proceeded to strut down to the end of the football field by the new boy's house. There was a crowd enough down there for me to get the attention that I wanted. I really didn't want any one's attention except the new boy's. Gill was his name. What kind of name was that for a black boy? When we first saw them moving their furniture into the apartment, we knew they had come from another cut of cloth. I guess that shows you that, you never know when you just might have to come down a notch and maybe even return to the hood in your life. I was curious to see if he was gonna be a better friend to me than Jeremy. Maybe…he could help me forget Jeremy?! Well, I will worry about that later. I just needed him to see me in my birthday suit. I got a new stroll about myself as I got closer. When I knew I had their attention, Malcolm yelled to me, "You can carry yo po tail right on back down that sidewalk! Didn't nobody call for you down here." By that time, I was just about to round the corner to twitch my little, tight, yellow shorts around the other sidewalk so he could see me from behind, as well as he had when I was coming towards him. When Malcolm yelled at me, I just sashayed on with my head held high, and with much attitude. I fell right into the hole in the corner of the sidewalk! My ankle twisted, sunglasses went one way, and, I went the other! The guys all laughed me to shame! Then, something happened. Malcolm jumped up to see was I okay? Then, he marched over to Gill, and punched him straight in his face! He told him, "You don't get to laugh at my little sister! You ain't in with us like that yet!" Gill was so shocked he couldn't even rise up to defend himself! Everybody respected Malcolm. None of them said a word! Malcolm just grabbed me by my waist and told me to hang on. I limped along side of him, as he fussed at me. Who do we see coming up the sidewalk? That's right, Nadine! I tried to yank myself free from Malcolm's grip. I told him I could make it from there. He just did an about- face and headed back to the football field. I stumbled a bit as I got my new balance. Nadine staggered straight up in my face and started ranting at me! "Yo little hot ass got just what you needed! You didn't think nobody saw you wiggle yo behind down there by them manish tail boys did ya? Well, me and L.B. sat rat thur in the cah and watched just to see how fah you was gonna go." I couldn't stand the stench of her breath any longer! I tried to break past her and run off limping to get away from her. She yelled, "Run yo little fast self on to Jazzy, she gone beat that ass when ya get thur anyway! You ain't got nobody fooled but ole Miss Fancy Pants Tyler!" I yelled back at her, "You just jealous Nadine, just jealous! This is MY party Nadine…not yours!" I ran in the house, straight to my grandma, fell upon her and started crying like a baby! That was the longest and worse day I had had since Dummy died! All of the kids that had nothing to do with me, or Delores for that matter, showed up to try and get in on the goodies. I made it clear to Jazzy that I was not having it at all! "If I don't give you a party hat….you couldn't be at my party!" Jazzy was cool with that. She didn't want the extra mouths to feed anyway. Delores was given one half of the cake with her name and designs on it, get this….she had the nerve to have Cinderella decorations on her half! She was far from that! I had Mickey Mouse crap on my side. At that point I didn't even care about a cake. I just didn't think she was worthy of sharing my money! All of the older kids hogged the hot dogs and chips. They did the nasty grinding and dips when the slow songs were played. And we had to act like we didn't notice too much, or, we would get pinched on the shoulder, or get our ears yanked on by the parents that were there! We weren't the ones doing the hunching, rolling and grinding! I will never forget my eighth birthday! When Jazzy finally had the money equally counted, gave Delores hers first, and put mine back in the jar, and gave it back to me, I took it, grabbed a chunk of cake from Delores' side of the cake, and ran up the Crepe! I stayed up there the rest of the evening rolling my eyes at Delores, and the rest of the kids. After all was said and done; Jazzy chewed my butt out for acting so selfish, and ugly to the guest. I didn't care. I was just glad it was over! Jazzy made sure I knew that it would be a long time before I had another party! I think I was really acting out because, Robby and Jeremy couldn't be there, and neither was my best friend, Dummy. They were away on vacation for the week of my party, but, Dummy was gone forever. Mrs. Tyler told me not to worry about splitting the money with Delores, because, she had something for me when she got back anyway. I itched with curiosity to know what it could be! I had to wait until it was time to go back to their house the following weekend! I gather my things for my trip to the Tyler's. I left with an excitement and a sag in my spirit. I was curious to know what Mrs. Tyler had for me, and sad because, there were no instruction to leave for Dummy anymore for the tree.

Chapter 9

Jazzy's Got Class Too!

When we pulled off from my house, Jazzy was still giving me that look to let me know that she didn't like the way I had acted, and was threatening to not let me go with them. I think she welcomed the relief of me going and not still pouting. On the trip over, we pulled into the parking lot of the local bank. Mrs. Tyler got out, opened the back door of the car and took me by the hand, and led me into the bank with her. I was dumb founded. She always took the boys in with her, and let me hang in the car with Mr. Tyler. Not today though. We sat down in the waiting area until this white man finished his business in the little office with the bank lady. Then, it was our turn to go in. I really liked the way Mrs. T talked to that white lady. She acted like she was just as smart, and had just as much money as she did. I was proud of her. That's just the way Jazzy talked to white people when she had to do business with them. So, I made a point to remember to do the same. Boy was I shocked when they finished their discussion! The white lady pulled out a little red booklet, and told me to come over and take a look at it. I looked at Mrs. Tyler, she nodded in approval. She showed me my name on the top of the page. Then my eyes must've gotten as big as saucers when I saw the $50.00 below it! That's right. She opened me my very own, Savings account! That was the birthday surprise! Man, I thought I was rich! You know, back in the 60's that was a lot of money for an 8 year old! I skinned and grinned, and was all nervous like I had won a million dollars! When the white lady was explaining to me how to keep record of the money the Tyler's would put in for me each time, I started to shed tears of joy as I looked at the pride it gave Mrs. Tyler to do this for me. I ran around the desk, and hugged her so hard, she started laughing and pulling me off of her, so th8e white lady could finish our business! She handed me the little, red logging book. I marched to the car with my head up so high and proud! The boys already knew what was going on. It turned out that Jeremy was still Jeremy. Robby gave me a hug of approval, and Jeremy, just shrugged his shoulders, and did the ole tooth sucking sound and said: "That ain't nothing we been had a bank account." Mrs. Tyler reached over the seat and popped him in the mouth so quick with the back of her hand, we both ducked! I knew not to laugh, because, that would mean more ill treatment from Jeremy once we got home! Mr. Tyler just mumbled...."Boy, you gone learn yet, when to keep yo mouth shut." He just sat there with his nostrils flaring, and breathing hard, and had turned that red color that he turns when he gets mad. Couldn't ***nothing*** burst my bubble that day! The first thing I wanted to do was, call Jazzy, and tell her my good news. But; Mrs. Tyler said she wanted to wait and surprise her at the right time. I needed to tell somebody! It had to be kept as our "little Secret for now". The magic of the moment faded fast after that. I did have to get up during dinner and hug her and Mr. Tyler again though. It felt very special to have some money in the bank as an 8 year old! Robby tried to tell me of the fun stuff they did on vacation. Of course, Jeremy shot down everything he considered fun, and called it "Corny". Why did he have to be such a "Butt Head?! He was not happy lately. So, no one else was gonna be happy when they were around him. That's if he could help it. I still wanted to hear what they did on their trip. I learned that there were some other cute cousins in their family! That's right. The pictures of their cousins from Atlanta! Whew! Baby, baby....Jeremy was slop compared to Tyrone! He was a bit older than them. But; you could tell that Mr. Tyler's brother, had it just like he did, if not better. They had some strong genes in their family! The boys and the girls were nice looking! Well, wouldn't you know it? Jeremy spotted me gazing at Tyrone's picture too long and started acting crazy with me and Robby, all over again! He had to include Robby, because, he didn't want to look too obvious, that it was aimed at me. This dude was driving me crazy! I didn't even like him that much anymore. Lies, all lies. Who was I fooling? I don't think there is anything he could've done to make me stop liking him!

He mellowed out a bit when it was my turn to tell them about my birthday party. I had to back up to where Dummy died while they were away. They didn't know him like that, but, they knew how I felt about him. You could tell they had been taught to care about the handicap and less fortunate people. They just gave me their undivided attention, and Jeremy even gave me a hug to show he was sorry for me losing my friend! Wow! If that's what it took to get him to be nice, I don't think I want his hugs! I'd have to keep losing my loved ones to get him to be kind to me! No thanks!

Saturday rolled around, and that meant wood hauling time for the men in the house. Mrs. Tyler told me we would be doing some girly stuff, so I would need to get all dolled up. This was my first real Tea party. I had played with my set that I got for Christmas, with my sisters and cousins, and dolls. This was totally different. We had to wear a certain length dress, gloves, and a strand of pearls on our neck, and we had to act like we didn't like each other that much, but had to be nice and proper anyway, at the beginning. This was odd to me, because, I was used to laughing loud, and cracking jokes on each other when we got together for anything around my folks. The thing that was weird about this is, all of these black women and their daughters were talking low, and thru their noses it seemed! They all sat up really straight and crossed their feet, instead of their whole leg, like I saw Jazzy, and Nadine nem do when they got together and drank their liquor. We had to sit to the edge of our seats, and place napkins over our laps, and try not to hold our little finger out, and sip our tea very quietly. There was no cussing or loud laughing like at Jazzy's house. I knew I was prettier than most of the little girls there, but, they looked at me like I stunk or something! I had to whisper in Mrs. Tyler's ear about it. She scolded me about whispering in her ear first. She said that wasn't, "polite." Then she told me that I should just ignore the girls and just follow her lead, whatever that meant. I was extremely bored, and feed up with having to act snooty! I wished that JoJo and L.B. were there to put those Heffas in their place! I was really mad about the food! They made us eat these thin, not sweet at all, ole crackers, with cheese sprayed on them from the can. We had to drink this hot, bitter tea, and the only good thing was the Butter mints! I was livid! I don't believe I played with my tea set but one time after that. That was just to show Deginna and my sister Sasha nem how they all acted there that day! We laughed a while at those snobs! I was put to shame when I tried to tell mama what happened. She let me know on all accounts that I was the one in the wrong! She had to show me how a Tea was really done! I was shocked to see that she knew every detail of what those ladies did, wore, and how they conducted themselves! She even showed me how to serve the tea, and when to drink, and not to! Oh, and don't forget the "pinky" finger thang! I was wondering why she never told me any of this before. Well, she let me know. "That's because, you never invited me to your lil Tea parties. That's why" I couldn't do nothing but, laugh, and hug her. I was so proud that she had all the sophistication, of Mrs. Tyler, and the other ladies, and knew how to do it with sassiness! I loved my mama! You know, the real kill was when she had to use JoJo and L.B. to make her point. She tried to get Nadine in on it. You already know, she was not a good candidate. She was happy to just stay as country as she was! Now on the other hand; them sissies delighted to show off! They had the "pinky" thing, just right. But, they were determined to cross their whole leg because, they both had on hot pants, (short, shorts) and wanted to flaunt their thighs! Jazzy had them putting on a show! We laughed, and kept asking for more tea, just to see L.B. cock all up when he poured it! Nadine just rolled her eyes at them, and shook her head. You could tell she wanted to laugh too. She got her chance to show off when Jazzy declared it was time out for the sophisticated stuff. She said it was time to "make it funky!" James Brown did a song titled that back then. That's all Nadine needed to hear! She jumped up, and started that old nasty dancing that she do each time that song, of many others would be played. Mama sent us out to play in the yard. She said it was the grown folk's party time now. We always welcomed that because, we knew we would get paid to dance again, go to the candy lady, and buy all the junk we could hold. Then, Raymond was gonna do his performance of James Brown, Malcolm was gonna put the sheet over him, and crown him the king of Soul, Dave would've come at that point, and started crying with drunk emotion, as Malcolm slowly placed the sheet on Raymond as he broke out in a “cold sweat”. Man, it was some real times on that corner in the Projects!

Guess who rolled up? Mrs. Tyler and the boys! She was running some errands, and stopped by to see if Jeremy and Robby could hang over until she came back? My heart was beating like that was my first time around them! I think I was shocked that she let them come to the Projects to be with our kind of company! You could have bought Deginna for a nickel. She was just blushing, and acting goofy. I tried to act like it meant nothing to me because; I see them all the time. Malcolm was glad to have some new company, in the form of males. He and Raymond always had to hang around us when the grown folk’s party went on. Mama wanted them right close to home when they knew they were gonna be drinking all day and night. That meant hanging under all females! You really couldn’t include JoJo and L.B.; they thought they were the “Girls” too! Well; Jeremy came over there with that cockiness. He didn’t know that Raymond lives for a reason to fight. Everything was going fine after we came back from the candy lady. Robby thought that was the coolest thing in the world to be able to go right in the hood to a place and get all the junk you wanted! They weren’t allowed to have candy, but every so often. We got back, did what it was routine to do. We poured all the candy in a pile, in the middle of the Indian style circle we sat in. We kept our pickles, each to ourselves in the little, brown bag. Robby prepared to do the same, and Jeremy yanked him by his arm, and told him; “Don’t you pour your candy on that nasty floor! You know they got roaches, and all these drunk folks over here dancing, probably done peed on it anyway!” It was like; somebody had slapped Raymond in the face. It smacked me too for that matter. Robby yanked his arm free, and poured the candy right on in with ours. As if it wasn’t already enough that Jeremy had said what he had; he got into the circle and kicked the pile all over the room! Raymond was on him before any of us could even grasp what had happened! Malcolm was ready for Robby, but Robby was charging for Jeremy too! The boys were laying it on Jeremy, while we were trying to find all the candy that had gone under the couch and chairs and the stereo table. That's what did it. We were trying to get under the stereo table, and the fight rolled that way at the same time. Mama nem didn't even know what was happening until then. At least, that's what I thought. The 45 vinyl that was playing did a loud screeeeeeeeeech, and the table came tumbling down! Everyone was there. All in the twinkling of an eye! Everything came to a halt. I know Jeremy was so glad! They put some flame on his butt! Raymond was huffing and puffing and standing there like he wasn't officially finished yet. Malcolm and Robby were buddied up, rolling their eyes at Jeremy. Everybody else just pointed at Jeremy. Mama walked over to Jeremy, we all knew this was really it. She threw her arm around his shoulders, and grabbed him close to her hips, and just laughed at him! She said, "Are you the one causing all of this commotion in here?" He just hung his head in shame, but, relief. She put her finger under his chin, and made him look at her. She told him, there were 2 things that she didn't play about, and that was her music, and her kids. "Do you understand?" He said, "Yes ma'am." She went to check to see if the stereo still worked, it did. She turned to Jeremy and told him, "I'm gone act like I didn't hear what you said about my floor, and my friends peeing on it since Raymond done already whipped yo ass real good, okay?" We all laughed like crazy! He couldn't do nothing but, laugh too. He was so happy he didn't get another beat down. Mama told him and Robby that that was as far as that needed to go. They knew that meant they didn't have to tell their mama when she got back. We all split the candy that we did find, and proceeded to play on like nothing ever happened. Now Raymond had to let it be known and understood that, we fights in the Projects when somebody put us down, or talk about where we live! Jeremy explained his bumps and bruises to Mrs. Tyler as football with the "Hood Kids". "They hit much harder than the guys at home!" She just told him it was good for him. It made him tougher she had said.

****

Chapter 10

Jazzy Gets Her Man!

The crisp, cool winds of autumn seemed to always manifest after the Fair made it to town. It was like magic to me! The weather would begin to do its thing when the smell of cotton candy, popcorn, and the funnel cakes filled the air at the State Fair. We would walk in large groups thru the projects, just before dark. The bigger kids looked out for the little ones. That was a time when everybody got along and it seemed like love was in the air. The teenagers that were couples, held hands, and hugged up on one another. Some of the girls sported the huge, stuffed animals their guys had won for them. We ate our cotton candy, slow and deliberately trying to make every bit last, as long as possible. We couldn't afford to ride many of the rides. We road what we could, walked around and jived with everyone we recognized from the hood, grouped together, and talked of our wish list for Christmas on the walk home.

Some things are just preludes to an era of your life that are more breathtaking than you ever imagined was possible. I didn't ever think I'd breathe again when I got the news about Dummy's death. He was allowed in our life to be our schoolmaster for what we would shortly experience as a family. We learned to sign, to communicate feelings, ideas, express intentions, and to let Dummy know that he was as much a part of our family as each of the many kids in the family at the time. He left this life, knowing that he was loved and accepted by all of us. What we didn't realize, was, he being in our lives was preparing us for the new love mama was about to encounter.

The military guy didn't come back anymore. Jazzy's sisters and my cousins eventually, moved out into their own places. We were living a bitter/sweet mood in the house at this time. It was too quiet! If me and Sasha didn't fight….it was a boring night. Jazzy read a lot those days. She seemed relieved to have her space, but, she seemed awful lonely. I watched her a lot. The routine of preparing for the holidays were slipping her. The excitement of getting the place all decked out was not there this time. We were gonna need a Christmas miracle!

I eased up on the bed aside mama. She never lifted her eyes from the page. "What you want Henny?" I just laughed. They called me that for a nick name at the time, because, there was a time when we were preparing for Easter. I was trying on my lil dress, so was Sasha. Miriam was in the kitchen, dying the eggs and getting the baskets and stuff ready. I was always the inquisitive one in the bunch. While Miriam had her back to me, I eased up to the table with my pretty, lil dress on. Jazzy was gonna have to hem it up a bit. So; while she was getting Sasha sized up, I had to go find out where baby Chicks came from, and how they got those different colors of fuzz for feathers from. Miriam was just singing, and dying eggs. The music was loud, and I was curious. "How do chickens lay eggs?" Miriam told me "Don't come in here with all them questions you be asking!" "Well, how they do it?" I needed to know. She said, "They just lay their chest down on the egg until the chick comes out." "Now leave me alone!" As soon as I knew she wasn't paying me any attention….I got the eggs that she hadn't boiled yet, put 3 of them under my chest, laid down on 'em good and hard on the table top, so they wouldn't roll away. That pretty lil Easter dress wasn't pretty no more! Crack! All 3 of them eggs was all over the front of my dress! Miriam turned around, gave me that look that said: "I knew, only you would pull this off!" She just grabbed a towel, grabbed me by the arm, and escorted me down the hall to Jazzy. You know, mothers just have this thing with them. I don't know how to label it. They just have it. When she saw the dress, all she said to Miriam was: "She tried to lay an egg didn't she?" I looked at Miriam to see how she would answer. Knowing all the time what she would say. "No, she tried to lay 3 eggs!" Sasha was like, "Ooooo, you gone get it now Monia!" She would've loved nothing better. Jazzy just laughed, said that we should have been expecting me to do that. She made me take the dress off, put it in the sink to wash, and went back to doing what she was doing to Sasha's dress. Sasha just walled her eyes at me because she wanted me to get a beating. Miriam warned me to stay out of the kitchen, and I did. I was too afraid to tempt Jazzy twice! So; that's why they started calling me "Henny".

I didn't want anything in particular. I just wanted to get up under Jazzy, smell her skin to see if she was still spraying Chanel no.5. If she was, she was still feeling like living. Well; she smelled Chanelish! You know, we may have ended up in the projects for a minute. But; mama was gonna at least try to keep us looking good and smelling like somebody! She would make that black bottle of perfume last a while! It was few and far times in between her getting another one.

I lay there on side of her quietly, as she read just looking at the ceiling. The phone rang, Jazzy sat straight up in the bed. She grabbed a cigarette, crossed her leg, and got that dreamy look in her eyes. She was talking real low, and doing that girlish laugh we females do when we want to charm a man. Who was this man? When did he see Jazzy to get our phone number? Why was she acting like she was so comfortable talking to him? I tried to act like I wasn't concerned about what she was talking about. The main thing is; I saw my mama smiling again! She was just sitting there in her slip and house shoes, stroking her hair, and twirling the end of a piece by her ear. There it was again, that lil girly laugh that she was doing! I tried to hang up under her until I found out about this man! She picked up on it. Without saying a word, she just gently took me by my arm, and led me out of the room. Man! I was trying hard to get the skinny on who this man was! I didn't want to ask Miriam, or anyone. I didn't want them in on my secret with mama. If she heard it from them, she might not let me come hang out in the room with her any more.

When she came to the front, she had this glassy look in her eyes like she was on a cloud. I had to ask her, "Mama, who was on the phone?" She just waltzed pass me, and said, "Oh, just a friend." He was more than a friend. I knew because, she didn't just say it. She sang it out. I just laughed inside with joy. Jazzy had a boyfriend. To see her perk up again, that was all that mattered to me. She got busy in the kitchen like someone was coming for dinner. My mind started to work a mile a minute! She had Miriam get the Living room spruced up, made me and Sasha get cleaned up for bed, and had Malcolm go to the back to watch TV We were all curious at that point. She didn't explain, she just kept us moving like little soldiers, getting the job done. I didn't dare start a fight with Sasha that evening. I didn't want anything to mess up the possible, "Boyfriend" for Jazzy. I didn't let it show that I knew a thang! I just figured that she would tell me all about it if I didn't blow her cover.

We got our baths; Miriam went across the street to Delores' house. Malcolm was closed up in his room. I loved it when Miriam left! That meant I could have her bed, and Sasha wouldn't be bugging me. I had to put plastic under the sheets when I got in Miriam's bed too. Yes, I was still wetting the bed....sometimes. Mama would let us read, or color until we had to turn the light off, as long as we were quiet, and didn't fight. I looked in magazines, and Sasha colored.

We both eventually fell asleep. I had to pee, so, I got up and ran to the bathroom. I always ran when I would get up on time, because, I was terrified of the dark! As I sat there with sleep in my eyes, I heard Jazzy in the front of the house talking with a man! I sat straight to attention. I normally would sit there like mama had told me to "Get it all out". She showed me how sometimes you have to pee twice. She was exactly right. This time, I didn't want to pee twice. I wanted to hear this strange voice again. I wanted to hear Jazzy laugh again. When I said she doesn't miss anything, she doesn't miss anything! She came down the hall, looked at me on the toilet, pointed to my room, and turned around without a single word. I knew that meant she wasn't even playing. It was hard for me to get back to sleep though. I was trying to strain to hear all I could. I knew one thing for sure, he talked soooo slow! He made my mama laugh though, and that made me laugh.

Morning couldn't come fast enough for me. I ran straight to mama's room. She was sleeping in that morning. I eased over on the other side of the bed, and got real close to her. I knew if she felt me there, she would wake up. Not this time. She was out! I moved, wiggled around a lot, and tried to cough a fake cough. It didn't work. Then I got scared! I shook her to see if she was ok. She was ok alright. She growled like a bear, and told me, "Get yo lil frail tail out my bed, and let me get some sleep!" I jumped, and took out of that room! I knew she had been up all night, because that's how she acted when her and Nadine had been out partying all night.

Malcolm was already in the kitchen eating cereal when I came up front. He didn't look up, or say a word to me. That wasn't unusual. I just got a bowl, and was gonna do the same. That is, until I reached for the box of "Quakes". He snatched it from me so hard he spilt his bowl and made me drop, and break mine! He yelled, "You gimme this box. Don't you see me reading it?" There went the quiet morning's sleep in for Jazzy. Not to mention, an ass whipping for me.

Jazzy came straight for me. She didn't ask no questions, she just had had enough of me disturbing her peace since the night before. Malcolm could do no wrong anyway….ever! He was the only boy, and he looked just like her. Not to mention, he was spoiled rotten! There was no point in even trying to build a case, or defend your case where he was concerned. Her baby boy could do no wrong. He just couldn't. I got one of those sitting downs that made your butt hurt worse than it already did from getting swatted. It's like you get thrown in the chair, instead of, placed in the chair. Mama poured me a portion (not quite enough in my opinion) of cereal, stormed back to bed, and I knew I better not try to get the box again to get anymore. I was pissed! Malcolm just sat there grinning behind the box like he thought I couldn't hear good or something. Then, who walks in but, Sasha. She took right up with Malcolm, laughing me to shame. I knew if I gave her what she deserved, I would get blasted again. I felt so out- numbered!

I had to figure out a way to get back in Jazzy's good graces so I could find out about this man! Well, that didn't take much effort. Miriam came home from her stay at Delores'. We got all of our chores done, only after a bit of arguing about who was supposed to do what. Mama told us that evening, while pressing me and Sasha's hair that she needed to talk to us about something very important. I knew exactly what it was. I didn't say a word. Miriam was looking bewildered. Malcolm was his same passive self. Sasha was busy jumping around like a bug, trying to get mama to tell us what it was NOW. Mama just laughed, and told us we would just have to wait until she finished frying the fish and fries we typically had on the weekends. The difference this Saturday was the fact that we had to put on some of our better clothing. Miriam was all for that because, she liked an occasion to dress up. Malcolm didn't want to do that because, he still wanted to go out and play until the street lights came on. This was the one time that Jazzy made him do what we had to do. I made it my business to tease him about it. I was still mad at him from the morning.

We didn't eat on paper plates that day. Jazzy got the pretty salad bowls down, and the bread saucers, and all of the good plates out. We knew that someone was coming. Well; he came. Boy was he handsome! He was a pretty brown skinned, slightly tall man. Guess what? He had freckles just like me! I had never seen anyone else that was black with freckles before now. I couldn't do nothing but, stare at him. He knew why I think. He just gave me a little wink and tapped his nose. He had them all over his nose just like me! Sasha acted kind of stand offish with him. Miriam was grinning about every little thing he said or Jazzy did. I was following Miriam's lead. She was as happy as I was that mama had a new friend and she was acting alive again. It seemed like the fish tasted better than ever before. The salad was crispier, and tasted like it was fresh from the garden. Everything seemed new! His name was Peter. When he said his name, it was like he sang it. We laughed because, he talked so slowly. Jazzy knew that we would find that funny. I think she liked how he talked. He told us that he had two little girls too. I wanted to know why he didn't bring them with him. He told us that if we would like that and would let him come back over again, he would bring them the next time. We all assured him that he could come back over again. That is, all of us but Malcolm. He didn't have much to say the whole time Peter was there. He ate his food with lightning speed, and ran to his room, and slammed the door. Mama didn't act like it bothered her in the least bit. Peter, however; looked a little bit hurt. Miriam told him, "Don't worry about Malcolm, he don't like nobody getting too close to Jazzy." We all laughed about it, and kept on talking. By the time we had finished eating, we all felt like we were gonna pop! Mama let me have as much Kool Aid as I wanted, and Sasha was a French fry eating fool! She loved French fries. Miriam didn't mind helping with the dishes this time. I knew then that having Peter in our life was gonna be a plus. If Miriam was happily doing the dishes....that was a miracle in itself. The two things she hated most was, helping to shampoo me and Sasha's hair, and washing dishes!

Chapter 11

Peter's Pride and Joy

Jazzy and Peter went to the living room and put on some music, drunk their beer, and sat real close to each other. I hadn't seen my mama with but one man that I could remember. That was that military guy. I didn't even see them together really. I just know he came in the bedroom, and I could hear what sounded like closeness. This just felt right, and good. To have a man in our house gave me the hope that we could have just what the Tyler's had.

Peter began to come over more. He even would work on his car in the front yard when he would come over. He would always bring bags of food, and something for us when he came. I didn't even want to go to the Tyler's on the weekends anymore because I knew Peter was gonna be over. It was odd for us the morning we got up, and Peter was sitting at the kitchen table while Jazzy was cooking bacon and eggs and stuff. Miriam was like a little girl again when he was around. Everything Jazzy asked her to do, she was right on it! Malcolm really tried to kick against the program. He tried to do whatever he thought would make Peter uncomfortable. Well, this morning, Jazzy had had enough! She called all of us down the hall into Malcolm's room. She made us sit down on his bed, and she looked us all directly in the eyes. This is what she said: "Now look; y'all know I love y'all more than life itself. I would kill for each one of y'all. There's no way that I would let anyone come up in here and do anything to hurt either of you. Now, this man in there is a good man. He is a decent man, and a church going man. I like him, no; I believe I love him. I wanted some happiness in my lonely life, and I wanted someone to come along side of me to be good to y'all too. That's what Peter wants to do, and dammit, I'm gonna let him!" "Malcolm, I know I told you that you were the man of the house, and I wanted you to help me look out for your sisters. Well; now you won't have to work so hard at it. I believe I've found you some help." That was the last thing Malcolm wanted. He liked being able to boss us around. Jazzy saw that look in his eyes that said so. "Malcolm, I'm still gonna need you to look out for your sisters, and I'm still expecting you to be a man about your business too. But; I'm not gonna have you thinking that you can tell me how to run mine too. You have got to trust me, and know that, I know how to handle mine. I wanted love, now I have someone to love not just me, but y'all too. Peter has two beautiful daughters, and they will be here sometimes too. I want y'all to treat them the way I treat y'all. It may be hard at first to get to know them, but, with a little love and patience from everybody; we can have a good thing here. Now, y'all know, I have taken in all kinds of folk, and there was always enough food, and love to go around for everybody, right?" We all said in unison, "Yeah." Jazzy corrected us of course. "Yes." We all laughed because, she was talking to us with bad grammar already! When she knew we had gotten the point….she gave each of us a hug that melted all of our hearts. Then she did something strange. She called Peter to come back in Malcolm's room. When he did, she looked him dead in his eyes. "Now Peter, I just had a good long talk with my kids. They know, I love 'em, and will kill the fool that tries to hurt either of them. I told them, I believe in you and me, and what we could have. I told them, you want to be there for us, and bring your baby girls into our lives too. Now, I don't want you making no liar out of me. These, right here, are my heart and soul. I won't let them disrespect you, and I ain't gone have no mistreatment of them from you. Now, are we gonna do this thing or what?" Peter came over to where we were sitting, and asked each of us, individually, "Do you want me to be in you and your mama's life, and have a family with y'all, and my girls?" We all quickly responded, that is, except Malcolm. He put his finger to his head, and then to his mouth, as if; he was in deep thought. All of a sudden, he lunged forward and grabbed Peter and hugged him so hard, and started crying! We were shocked! He told him he was sorry for being mean to him, and how he had always wanted someone to want to be his daddy. By then, we were all crying including Peter! I had not seen Jazzy cry since that time that Mrs. Tyler wanted to adopt me! This was a good cry. We all hugged, and dried up, went to the front, and had Kool Aid, and mama nem had a beer. We talked about the changes that would need to be made, and jazzy laid the law down about us telling anyone about the business that went on in her house! We already knew she didn't play that. When she was sure we were clear on everything, she told us to go outside while we still had some daylight. We took out the door, happy and fulfilled like we hadn't been in a looong time!

Peter kept his word. He brought his daughters over to meet us. I was breathless! I thought that the breath was all taken away when Dummy left me. Well, it happened again. Veronica was the splitting image of Peter! She just didn't have the freckles, and she was pale! Pale to the point of almost looking a yellowish, pink complexion, and had this dusty, red hair. She had the puppy dog eyes just like Peter. You know that almost sad droopy look in 'em. We thought that Peter talked slow. Veronica talked like she didn't have no kind of drive about herself. She wasn't unfriendly. She just acted like, she could careless whether you made her your friend or not. We were already used to that type of attitude in the hood. That's the way you had to act with the people there, at least until you got to know what made them tick. She would fit right in around here.

Now Jessica, that's who took my breath away. She never said a word at first. She just held on to Peter's leg like they were attached at birth! Now, that's who looked like the true version of Peter! Minus the freckles, she was a mini copy of him. Then something happened. Peter told Veronica to take Jessica to the bathroom, and help her to get cleaned up for dinner with us. Veronica began to do SIGN LANGUAGE for Jessica!! My mouth dropped wide open! Jazzy just reached over, and pushed my chin upward, and told Sasha, "Don't you say a damned thang." I knew that went for me too. Miriam was all excited about this! Malcolm was looking at mama like he couldn't believe she had gone and let another Mute come into our family! Peter picked up on Malcolm's reaction. He was generally a calm man, but, we learned that evening that, Peter was just like Jazzy about his kids. He walked right up to Malcolm, and asked him straight out; "Do you have a problem with Jessica, or something?" I mean he was right in his face! Jazzy didn't bulge to say a word. Malcolm didn't know what to do, or say. He had not had that kind of confrontation from a man before. That was a common thing for the boys in the hood to do, but, not a man that mama had in her company before. Malcolm looked at Jazzy.... she looked at him like, "What?" He dropped his head, and told Peter, there was no problem, and he was sorry. Jessica was a lil bitty thing. You could tell she wasn't as shy as she let on. As soon as she saw that Veronica was comfortable with us, she came to life. She proved to be, feisty, mean and bossy as any little girl I'd met. That is, except, Sasha. I knew I would be getting it from both ends now. Oh, I was just gonna have to see about this. I was not about to be bossed around by a kid that was way younger than me! That panned out right away after she learned that I could communicate with her so well. When I said that Dummy coming into our life was a fore shadowing of what was to come.....well; that's exactly what it was.

Jazzy had cooked Red beans, and rice, baked chicken, corn bread, and cherry, Kool Aid. Man, we ate like it was the "Last Supper"! Those girls could eat! Jessica must've been tired when she came because, she stuffed her face to the point of popping, then she started going to sleep at the table! We all got a good laugh out of watching her slowly leaning and swaying to this side and that side, and eventually; she just plopped her head forward onto the table. Even Peter didn't have a problem with us laughing at her on this one

This felt so good having a family with new sisters, going to church on Sundays, having a daddy that really felt like my own. The freckles really made it seem like he was my own personal daddy. I felt safe, and the future was looking brighter each day. Veronica was so happy to come over on the weekends, and Jessica was fast becoming so attached to Jazzy that she would push us back if we got too close to her. Forget about trying to get, or give Jazzy a hug. She actually had temper tantrums if Jazzy gave her own kids too much affection! This was soon getting on Miriam's nerves. She was past the age of needing all the hugs that me and Sasha were used to getting. Still, it made her somewhat ticked off to see that this new child addition to our family had come in throwing her weight around with everybody, including her mama! Jazzy took it all in stride. She had to explain to us around the Thanksgiving holiday, that Jessica acted like that because they had a bad life at home with their mom, and they were reaching out for the love they weren't getting at home. Of course, I wanted to know, why didn't they just come and live with us all the time. She just gave that expression like, "Who knows, they just might."

Mrs. Tyler was getting concerned that I wasn't coming over as much. She called to speak to me the week of Thanksgiving. I found it so hard to tell her that I would be spending Thanksgiving with my family. I could tell she was very saddened by it, because, she just got really quiet. I just began to tell her about the way things were feeling to me, to have Peter and his kids over. She listened to my whole story, then, she said the coldest thing I had ever had said to me. She told me that no matter how much I was enjoying it for now, the feel good wasn't gonna last for long, because they were living in sin. I didn't quite know what to do with that information

I know it didn't feel good for her to be telling me that the joy I was getting from Peter and my new "Sisters" being in our lives was gonna be short lived. I told her I had to go. That was the first time that I didn't want to be a part of the Tyler's world anymore. I didn't want to stay away always, at first. I just wanted to let the newness of Peter and my mama's happiness settle down some. This conversation with Mrs. Tyler had changed something in me though. I didn't fully understand what she meant by them "living in sin", I just know the way she said it sounded, cold and mean. It was as though, she didn't like their being together, because it kept me from coming over to be with her as much anymore. I knew I still loved her, but, I loved being with my "new family" more. I didn't even know how to tell Jazzy about what we discussed. I didn't want her to be mad at Mrs. T., nor, did I want her to feel the way I was just made to feel. I was feeling sick in the stomach when I hung up. I eased out of the house to my tree before Jazzy had the chance to ask me about the phone call. I sat out there as long as I could, and let the cold wind blow on my face to help me feel better. Times like these made me wish my grandmother was out there sweeping the sidewalk off so I could talk to her about all of this.

Chapter 12

This feels so Right!

Jazzy had the "Spirit" again. That is, the spirit of the holiday. She had the oranges, and earth tone colors sprayed around the house between the kitchen, and living room. She put out baskets of fruit and nuts to display and had cinnamon, and orange slices simmering on the stove in a little pot. That meant it was officially on for the holiday when you smelt the oranges and cinnamon sticks going on the stove. Peter brought a huge turkey from his job at the paper company. My auntie gave us a really pretty ham from her job. The store owner had done that for years for my auntie and mama each Thanksgiving or Christmas. He just needed to know ahead of time, which one they preferred. Jazzy sat there picking her collard greens to put up for the meal. She was in such a good mood these days. It started to rub off on us. The arguing was down. We did our chores together without falling out with each other. Veronica, and Jessica were not gonna be over until Wednesday. This way they would be able to stay up with us all night like we do, and help mama with the cooking, I really enjoyed the part of the cake making, when it was time to lick the beaters, the spoons and the bowls. That was one of my favorites. The smell of the cornbread baking for the dressing, the smell of the turkey baking, and the Sweet Potato pies, well, they just smelt like Heaven! Mama used to pull the turkey neck and gizzard out and we would sit there and eat it together after we put the dressing in the oven. I enjoyed all of the different, weird, crazy feeds she taught me to appreciate. My friends said I would try anything! Not anything, but, a lot of things. I would eat Cottage Cheese, and Peaches, when everyone else would be enjoying Jell-O. Sasha always rolled her pop eyes at me, because, the things that would make her gag, if she even smelt them, were the things that got me close to Jazzy by liking them. There was always that pull for the "Spot" with us. Sasha always wanted to be the center of attention, and I always had to show her, it wasn't always about her! That was always fighting material for us. As I said; it didn't take too much to jump one off. It was like, our sleeping pill or something. Then, when Veronica and Jessica came over, that was another battle for Sasha! She had to show, she was the baby in the family, no matter who it cut! Well, she had her hands full with Veronica too. That child wasn't red and dusty for nothing! You know how most girls just swing wildly into the air, with their eyes closed when they fight? Remember? Well; Veronica was like me. She fought like the boys fought. Eyes wide open, looking for where she could jab you next! It didn't bother her if you got a swing in on her. She just wanted to make sure that she hurt you, before she let go of you! I was so glad that someone had come along to put Sasha in her place, so I wouldn't keep getting a whipping after whipping her butt!

Jazzy didn't care if you were not her child when she kept you over to her house. If you acted a fool on her time, you got some act right in you on her time. The funny thing about that was, the kids always wanted to come hang out at our house! I believe they liked the company of L.B. and JoJo, not to mention when Nadine came over! It was like a circus at our house! Jazzy had already schooled her buddies about wanting to come and hang around all day when Peter came over. I heard her fussing at her friend Patsy one day. Patsy was very jovial, yet tomboyish, and loved a good brawl. She reminded me of a teddy bear, because she always brought comfort to us when she was around. Well, Jazzy had to let her know that, no man wants to come home to look at a house full of folks when he got off work. Patsy tried to argue that, this wasn't his home no way! Jazzy made it very clear, if he was paying bills up in there, and feeding and clothing hers; he could call it home if he damned well pleased! That was the first time I heard Jazzy talk to Patsy like that! Patsy was the one that had to talk reason with Jazzy when she had had too much to drink, and wanted to fight whoever was available. Patsy was the one that kept us in line, and made sure we had what we needed until Jazzy got through partying. So, my feelings were really hurt for her when Jazzy told her that. Usually, Patsy, and JoJo would clash when they were over to see us. I think it was because, JoJo tried so hard to be girly, and Patsy, being on the tomboyish side, always tried to bully him out. But, when it came down to the block bullies trying to start a humbug against JoJo and L.B.; they were as thick as thieves. Patsy would go to bat for both of them! Jazzy made her point, and Patsy started for the door. I thought she would try to call Patsy back. I became more certain with each passing event, that Jazzy said what she meant, and meant what she said about hers. She felt me looking at her, and snapped around real quick, and told me, "And, don't you be looking at me like that, feeling all sorry for her and shit". "Sometimes you just gotta put folk in they place about trying to run ya damned business for ya"! I realized she had a good point, because, Nadine told her what she needed to do, and ought to do all of the time. Whenever Jazzy told her what she needed to do....of course, Nadine cussed her out, and told her to mind her own damned business. I was still having a problem trying to figure out, how it is that, they cuss, and fuss with each other every day! Yet, they were the flip and the flop to each other's life. I didn't get it.

Patsy always knew how to get back on Jazzy good side. The next day, she came over and had a box of Christmas ornaments, and candy canes. Jazzy being the woman she was, received them with a kind spirit. I just watched out the corner of my eyes, across the room. I knew I didn't want to be called out again for putting my little gestures of two cents in. I got my checking the day before. They had their little talk and were back on track.

Peter came over, and had Veronica and Jessica with him. We were really feeling the spirit then. Mama got busy getting dinner ready for Peter, and Patsy got the hint, and got up, and eased on out. Jazzy had set things in order. She had us fed and out the way, and was ready to get down to the business of the Thanksgiving dinner. We expected to be up late that night to help with our part of the cooking. I believe we were more in the way, than helping. But, I know it made Jazzy have a good time to have all of us around her in the kitchen. I think the part that I hated the most was to have to peel the sweet potatoes, and the potatoes for the potato salad. It seems that me, and Malcolm always got stuck doing that part! Miriam got to help make the pies, and dice up the onion, celery and bell pepper. There was an aroma in the air just from doing that, that always made me hungry. Peter got his food down, got a beer, headed to the bathroom to take a bath, and left the rest up to us. Veronica called Jazzy, Jazzy. I always felt a twinge inside when she did. It was like she seemed somehow, equal with the other grownups that called her by her first name. So; you know I had to question it. I asked mama why she was allowed to call her by her first name, like Nadine nem did. She explained that, that was what she was supposed to do since, she wasn't her mother, and she hadn't been taught better by her mother. Well; I felt like somebody better get to teaching her because, I didn't like her disrespecting my mama. What better time to handle this than now. "Veronica, you are gonna have to start calling my mama by her right name, or you gonna have to stop coming over here". Mama stopped in midair as she was placing a pile of collard greens in the pot. "Monia, didn't I tell y'all, I know how to handle my business in this house? You not paying one bill up in here, to be telling nobody whether they can come or go. Do I make myself clear or not?" I tried to get away with the silent treatment. I just dropped my head, and kept on peeling the sweet potatoes. "Do I make myself clear or not"? "Yes." Veronica just waited long enough for Jazzy to turn around, and gave me this indignant look, and licked her tongue out at me, and gave me the middle finger! I was so proud of Sasha in that moment. She reached out, and grabbed Veronica's finger, and bent it back as far as she could, and told her, "You don't be shooting my sister the bird!" Mama turned around to see what all of the commotion was about, and pointed at me, Sasha, and Veronica, and then pointed towards the other room. No words exchanged, just that look, and the pointing of the finger. We knew we had better not say a word, but, just get out of her presence. I was ready to fight, and so was Sasha. I sat in the chair in the living room where I could see if mama was coming or, not. Sasha sat close enough to Veronica on the couch where she could punch her, and straighten up before she could be found out. When I gave her the "eye", she would jab Veronica. This happened 3 times, and Veronica didn't say a word. The next time Sasha got the "eye", reached out to jab Veronica, and straighten up....Veronica grabbed Sasha's fist, and twisted her whole arm so fast, and so hard that it made me leap from my seat, made Sasha scream for dear life, and I was on her! Peter came down the hall with the towel wrapped around his waist, and no shirt or shoes, Jazzy came from the kitchen with the wooden spoon she used to stir the sweet potato batter for the pies. Peter grabbed me, and Jazzy grabbed Veronica. This was a first. You could see the look of awkwardness on both of their faces. They were ready to deal with the other's child about messing with their child. This was not good.

Everyone was in the living room by now. Everyone was looking to see what the outcome was gonna be. Mama knew it, and so did Peter. They both said in unison “Both of y’all, go to bed!” Once again, Sasha was off the hook. Man, I couldn’t stand that girl!

When we got down the hall, I got in Miriam’s bed, and Veronica sat on the floor. Jazzy came down the hall into the room, and wanted to know why Veronica wasn’t on the bed. She told Jazzy, “I don’t want to sleep in the bed where Sasha sleeps.” “Why not?” “Because, she started this fight, and y’all let her stay in there with y’all like she all special and stuff”. This was news to Jazzy because, she thought, I started the fight. Veronica told her how it went down from the kitchen table, up to that point. Jazzy marched down the hall, and grabbed Sasha by the arm Veronica had already twisted, slung her onto her bed, and told her, “You get yo lil yellow ass up there, and go to bed too!” She put that infamous finger out, gave Veronica that infamous look, Veronica obeyed, got up on the bed with Sasha as close to the edge of the other side as possible, and cried herself to sleep. Me, and Sasha had to give each other confirmation that we had accomplished enough of our plan to put her in her place around there as needed. I nodded at her, and she stuck her thumb in her mouth, and threw her head up high, and pulled all of the cover she could to herself, turned her back to Veronica, and covered her head.

You know what made me feel so bad about it all? The same sad cry that I had heard Dummy cry, the day the kids had jumped him on the church ground, was the same sad cry I heard from Jessica when she saw how we did Veronica. It was so pitiful! She took it so hard to see her sister crying at a place that we were supposed to be making them feel loved, and making a family work.

As I lay there trying to go to sleep, I kept wondering how Thanksgiving was gonna be now that this had all happened. I knew that it would be my fault if it was bad the next day. I tossed and turned trying to get to sleep. I got up, went to the bathroom. I tried to make noise so mama would come down the hall and see what it was. I knew if I could just get her to come, I could explain that, I just wanted Veronica to respect her. I felt she would understand, I could apologize to her, and Peter, and things would be ok. Well, she did come. I did explain, and she told me to go talk to Peter, and maybe, he would forgive me. Well, he did understand, and told me about how, Veronica's mom didn't even make them call her mama! They called her by her first name too. That's why she called Jazzy by her first name. I asked him why Jessica sounded like that when she cried, and why she took it so hard. He looked very sad when I asked him that. He told me that there was always a lot of fighting in their home, and their mom, beat them a lot too.

I made up in my heart that night, that, I was not going to ever be mean to them again. I was just heartbroken to learn this. He told me that Jessica's voice pipe, as they called it back then, was not well, and that was the reason her cry sounded that way. I told him I was really sorry again, went to bed, and you know what? I was able to go to sleep then.

I felt like we were whole. Waking up with Peter, and his daughters, on Thanksgiving, wow! We had our breakfast, and watched the annual parade. Peter wanted it to hurry up and be over, so he could watch the football game. Malcolm looked forward to watching the games with Peter. Because, Peter could call all of the plays before the Ref could even get the whistle in his mouth good! We all thought that Peter was just what mama needed, because, he was smart about different things that most people had no clue about, just like she was. He had a really gentle way of teaching you about stuff. Not with the cockiness that some grownups tried to handle you with, because you didn't know a certain thing, about a certain matter. He was patient with us. He didn't even mind all the questions I had about the running of a car. He would answer all 121 of them, then, tell me to go ask mama a question for him, that there was no answer to. This was his way of putting the task on her, of my inquisitiveness; without pushing me away, or acting like I was a bother. As I got older, it hit me that, that's indeed what he was doing, when he would send me to ask her! That's what I call, "Clever Love", and that's how he did most things that he did for us.

Mama had put the rolls in the oven, and the Pecan pie was just out of the oven. The smell made you want to bite a big chunk out of it right then, and there! The roasted pecans and the sweet savor of the molasses, and the crust all blended into a whirl in my nostrils! I thought I was gonna die if I didn't get a piece fast enough!

Peter said the grace so good, it made me and mama cry tears in silent. It was like you could feel God touching you with love, while he was praying. He thanked God for all the many things he had done for him, and us. He thanked him for blessing him with a family that loved him. He even added "finally" on the end of that part of the prayer. I saw him in a better way each time he came around. I knew that a man that prayed like that was a good man indeed. That led my mind to wondering, why could Mrs. Tyler say that mama was not gonna be blessed for being with Peter

All of the food was so good! We ate, and ate, and ate! I think the joy of us all being together, made us happy eaters. It wasn't long that everyone had found a place to flop, and we all were snoring before long. That was a Thanksgiving to remember for many years to come. Malcolm and Peter had the drum sticks, and Miriam and me had the wings of the turkey. Mama and Jessica wanted the dark meat, and Veronica and Sasha tore in to the breast meat. Jazzy did that turkey like none she had done before. I think she was trying to show out for Peter. I liked it when she fed him from her plate, and he fed her pie with his hand. She was so happy with him being there with us!

After we all came back to life from our nap, we all piled into Peter's car and went to find a Christmas tree. There was this place called the Civic center. When we drove by it, there was Christmas lights strung everywhere! It was so pretty! We went to all of the lots in town to find a tree. None would satisfy Jazzy. So, we rode around to watch all of the lights in the white folk neighborhood. The next day, Jazzy and Peter left us at home with Miriam in charge. When they got back, they unloaded this box from the car. Inside, there were a lot of shiny, fluffy branches of an aluminum Christmas tree! They put it together, and had us pass them each branch. After every branch was put in place, they opened another box. Inside of this box was a colorful light that spin around, and around and all of the different colors flashed on the branches of the tree! It was like magic! My eyes were locked on the tree for what seemed like hours! I didn't care if I got nothing else for Christmas. The time we spent putting the tree together, seeing the lights, and listening to the music Jazzy played while putting the tree together, as we sipped the Eggnog she had made. There was nothing to take the place of that moment. I placed that day in my head to keep forever.

Chapter 13

The Last Dance

The wet, cold days of winter kept us inside a lot. This made for a lot of arguing, and fighting among the 6 kids in the family now. If it wasn't me and Sasha, it was Veronica and Sasha. I tried to hang in Malcolm's room and play marbles with him. If I won his Tiger's eye, or Black Marley; he would put me out if I tried to play for keeps. I always made the point that I thought that we were playing "keeps". Of course, he had his own set of rules when you beat him out of his favorites. Malcolm asked me something that surprised me. I never thought he cared much about what concerned me, unless someone in the hood tried to fight me. Well; I was wrong. He wanted to know why I haven't been back to the Tyler's in so long. I had a couple of answers. One being, I didn't like the idea that Mrs. T. had suggested that, mama and Peter's relationship wasn't gonna be blessed because, they weren't married. Secondly, I had always wanted the feeling of family. Now we had it with Peter and the girls being there with us. So; I didn't need to be over to the Tyler's to get that anymore. I still loved her, and the boys especially Jeremy. I thought that I was being selfish, or that I had kinda used them until times got better at my house. But, in essence; they had used me for their consolation. After all; it was Mrs. Tyler that needed me to come to be the lil girl she never had anyway. That's how I reasoned with myself about it all. Malcolm agreed with my views about it, and was sort of pissed with

Mrs. Tyler too for saying all of the things she did about mama and Peter. He agreed that I needed to stay from over there for a while too. Deep inside though, I missed being over there with them....sometimes. It dawned on me that Malcolm was just trying to get my mind off the fact that I had taken his favorites, and get this; he had eased them all back while we were talking! I couldn't do nothing but laugh, and concede. I was just glad that he had allowed me in his room to play with him in the first place. He could be very grouchy sometimes....well; a lot of times. I was also glad that he had showed concern for me, and; sided with me.

There was a lot of buzz around school, because it was time for our winter dance. We called it "The Social". Everyone was excited because this was the one time that they allowed the big kids and the kids from the lower grades to be together. We were always curious to see who was gonna be in a corner somewhere, hugged up kissing, or who was gonna win the dance contest this time. It was a given that, Raymond and Malcolm were gonna win the boy's contest. They always did. It didn't matter where the dance contest was held...they were gonna bring home the trophy. Raymond danced in his sleep! Malcolm just had this cool about his dance style that came so natural, no one could deny him. JoJo and L.B. coached us year around on dance techniques. JoJo had already warned us that someone better come home with a trophy! We were ready! Raymond and Malcolm had fresh haircuts, their shoes were polished, faces greased down. Raymond had his pimp walk on, and Malcolm had on his cool. Miriam and Delores had gotten their group together, made up some moves, had outfits that matched, and JoJo had danced them so hard during rehearsal times, their legs were wobbling when they finished! He was going to the dance to make sure they did all of the moves just right. He took this thing serious! Mama and Nadine would stay home, play their rounds of music, drank beer, and wait for the word from JoJo to say who came close to, but couldn't beat us call.

The school across the bridge from our school was known for starting fights at the Social. They went for bad in school, and out of school. If you were not from their hood, and dated a girl from their hood, you better be nice to her. If you didn't....you had to take a beat down when you went back to see her! There was a cat that I called, Ole Dude over there. He was big, black as the night, and mean as hell! He didn't say much to anybody. When he came to our side of town, he would just stalk through the neighborhood, stop and watch the guys playing football, and me too when I played with them. He wouldn't say a word! He always gave me that lil knowing nod that let me know he thought it was cool that I was tough enough to play with the big boys. I just looked at him, and tried to keep my tough face on. He knew I was trying to keep from blushing with pride. It said a lot for him to approve of anything! His sister was in the 6th grade, and she looked as mean as him, and she was! She hadn't been moved to the school across the bridge yet. They did that after they graduated from the 6th grade. I will be forever grateful to her for rescuing me! I always played with boys, so, I didn't know that they picked on you, pulled your hair, and said embarrassing things about you in front of their boys, to show they liked you! I spent so much time trying to like Jeremy, that I never knew that any boy that I played with at school, or from the hood ever noticed me to like ME! Well; there was one. I shall never forget the whipping he put on me! I thought I could hang with the least and the greatest of them, in fighting and football. I have to confess….Danny beat me silly! When I thought I could not take another punch; Janice showed up out of nowhere, pulled him off of me, and yanked me up by one hand! When I finally could see straight, and breathe, she shoved me to the girl's bathroom, splashed water all over me, dried my face, looked me square in my eyes, and told me this: "If you ever let a dude beat you like that again, you gone have to fight my black ass, and you don't wanna do that!" She made me dry up and tell her what happened. I told her how he had been chasing me and pulling my hair all throughout recess. When I got tired of it, I swung on him, and ran. When I thought it was over, he slipped up behind me and sneaked me! That seemed to have met her approval, because she gave me credit for him sneaking me. Whew! That saved me. She made me hang out with her for the next few days at recess. She would sneak over to the lil kid's side of the playground to meet with me to plan how we would get Danny back. I felt so important, and safe.

Gotta get back to the Social! The dance was well underway, the contest still in preparing. Me, Deginna, Sasha, and Sharletta had our orders to stay together at all times! We knew we had better do just that. We ran the room to scope out all the smoochers at the dance. We knew we would find ole hot tail Janice posted up somewhere, with whoever. She had no shame. When she saw us, she just giggled, turned around, and took up where she left off, wrapping her lips around somebody we didn't recognize. We rolled our eyes among each other, shook our head, and ran on to the next corner. I was almost jealous, because, I wanted Jeremy to want to kiss me too. Well; we got back to the gym, where the stage was for the contest. They had the lil kids do their dance first. Then the double Dutch, rope dancers came out and did their number. That was so cool! Then came the big kids! Everybody got quiet, the music got louder, and everyone ran towards the stage to get a good look. JoJo was stuck like glue in the corner of the stage to clock Miriam and her group. When it was their turn, everybody got totally quiet, and all eyes were on JoJo. He did his quick hand clap, gave them that look that said: "Y'all Heffas better dance!" Everybody had intensity in their eyes, just like JoJo. We knew we had to show up the groups from across the bridge! Miriam, Delores, Jackie, Linda, and Dianne did that thang man! They whipped their hips; they strut their stuff, did their slides and pranced all over that stage! When they finished, they did a lil humph of their shoulders, and high stepped off the stage! The crowd went crazy!! JoJo pranced out, did a bow, and ran off the stage to the girls to praise them for a job well done! JoJo took his craft so serious he had tears of joy in his eyes when he got to them! They did all of the hand jive, and smacking their lips, and rallying around one another with laughter, screams, and hugs!! You would think they had won a million dollars each! The folks across the bridge knew it was already over for them after this. They didn't show any sportsmanship! They didn't even crack a smile, or clap, or nothing! They just stood there with their arms folded over their chest, and rolled their eyes at Miriam nem! If they were pissed off about this one; they were really gonna be mad about Malcolm and Raymond's Pimp Daddy dance routine!! Everybody in the hood turned out to see them dance! It was said that there hasn't ever been anybody to live there before we came to the projects that could dance like Jazzy, her kids and her sister's kids!! They even turned out the night clubs when her and her sisters went out clubbing! If Jazzy wasn't getting put out for fighting, they danced the night away!

Something was seriously wrong! While everyone was waiting for Malcolm nem to come on, there was a lot of screaming going on behind the stage area, near the back door! The people near the stage heard it first. Me and Sasha grabbed hands, and, Deginna grabbed Sharletta's hand. We knew we'd better come home together, or else! There was chaos out back!! It was dark but, you could make out the faces of the people you knew. Delores was laid out on the ground, like she was dead! Miriam was just pulling her long, jet black hair, and running in place screaming!

Raymond, Malcolm, and some of the other boys we played football with were piled up on top of somebody beating them to a pulp!! Things got really weird when, out the corner of my eye, I saw JoJo, doubled over, on the ground, clutching his stomach!! L.B. was down over him rocking and crying to the top of his lungs, begging someone to go get help, go get Jazzy!! Nobody could respond, because everybody needed attention! You didn't know who needed the most!! Sasha grabbed my hand, and we ran as fast as we could all the way home to get Jazzy, and nem!! We were so out of breath that we couldn't even get the words out right! Sasha was trying to tell her version, and all she could get out was, "JoJo.... dead!" I couldn't do nothing but, pull on Nadine's arm for her to come see! Jazzy called the police, and we jumped in Nadine's car, and sped back to the school. When we got there, mamas were running and scurrying all over the place trying to find their children. We didn't know where Deginna and Sharletta was, because, we had left them there. I got scared all over again. Mama made us wait in the car after we told her where everything was happening. We really wanted to go make sure Delores hadn't got trampled on, because she was still out cold when we left! Then the sirens came blasting thru the campus car after car, after car! Then the ambulance came. Our heads were spinning around like a spinning top! I didn't know there were so many police in our town! We couldn't stay in that car knowing that everyone we loved was in that building, possibly needing our help to fight! Sasha was thinking the same thing I was thinking. We grabbed the door handles at the same time. The noise, and the turned over tables and chairs, punch, and cake and shoes were everywhere! We couldn't find mama nem either. The principle was frantic! The next thing I saw dropped me to my knees! They went past us with someone on a stretcher that had a sheet over their face! The arm was all that was hanging off the side uncovered. I knew that arm anywhere. It had cradled me when I was afraid of the lightening, when I needed my hair combed, it had pulled my hair back in the tightest ponytails, and fought for me and my family many times. It was JoJo on the stretcher! Dead, and gone from our lives in a moment! When Sasha saw me fall, she knew that look, and that same stare was in my eyes when Dummy had left me. She just slid down the wall and sat beside me too. Neither of us was there anymore. Soon after that stretcher passed, we saw another one coming our way. I tried not to look, because I didn't want to know. From the corner of my eye, I saw it was Delores! She was alive, but her face was bloody. L.B. came running past us, and the whole crew from our household was behind him. When Nadine saw me and Sasha, she shot out some cuss words, scooped us up, and drug us to the car. We were dead weight because we felt dead inside. Malcolm and Raymond had to walk home, because the car was full. Mama was trying to keep a strong face up for us, but, it wasn't working. She was crazy about JoJo! He was like a lil brother to her, he idolized her, and she had such compassion for him because she saw his struggle every day! He wanted to be a man, because he wanted to father a son so badly. He wanted to be a woman, so he could be just like Jazzy. He was everybody's secret keeper, and cheerleader for every under privileged girl and boy in the projects. He let them know they could be anything they wanted to be, if they would hold their heads up and believe! We needed him!

Delores was gonna be fine. She just got trampled a bit. She was released from the hospital with a broken arm, and a heart ache. She took the news about JoJo as hard as the rest of us. Mama got so sick, with all the throwing up she did....she had to be taken to the hospital too. Nadine went ballistic and started a cussing and crying fit that no one could tame. We all took to our corners and cried until we couldn't anymore. Then everything got dead quiet. Peter came home from work, and got the news of JoJo and Delores, and mama. He was so pissed off that no one had called him to come help. He headed back out of the door to go see about mama.

When they came back from the hospital, mama had the strangest look in her eyes. It was not the look she left with. It was a look of joy, and sadness at the same time. If that is possible to have such a look, she had it. Nadine knew the look, because she knew Jazzy. She walked over to Peter, and said, "You sly dog you!" He laughed, and rubbed mama on the stomach. Even as young as we were, we knew what that meant. Me and Sasha started laughing and jumping around in a circle holding hands. Miriam ran to the back, slammed the door and started screaming like a crazy person. Malcolm looked at mama and asked her what it all meant. She smiled at him and told him. "You may be getting that lil brother you never had!" He looked back and forth at her and Peter, then blurted out, "Man, you done gone and got my mama pregnant?!" He ran into Peter swinging with all his might! Mama and Nadine had to pull him off of him. The amazing thing is that Peter, once again did not put his hand on Malcolm! Once mama got him calmed down, her and Peter had to talk to him, and Miriam. Malcolm felt like he was bringing shame on my mama and Miriam felt it was bringing shame on her before her friends. Of course, Nadine cussed both of them out. She already had 7 kids herself! She wanted mama to have a house full of kids just like her I guess. She went on ranting and raving about how God had blessed mama's womb, and how children were a blessing from the Lord. Miriam wasn't even caring about all of that. The only thing she could think about was, her friends making fun of her because her mama was the age she was and having a BABY!!!

Just as it would happen….Miriam got into a fight with, guess who? That's right, Delores! It started that morning on the way to school. She started teasing Miriam, and making the other kids laugh as she poked her stomach out and walking with her back all swayed, and knees bent like she was carrying the weight of the world on her shoulder. Miriam walked along quietly with her head held high, not saying a word. After school,

Raymond walked just a few steps behind her. Malcolm was responsible for walking me and Sasha home. Raymond was responsible for Deginna and his other brother and sisters getting home without problems. Delores had older brother and sisters that had gone on to high school and college. So; I don't understand why she would start a fight when she didn't have backup. She started talking the same mess she was talking before school that morning. But, that evening, she tried to put on a real show for her so called friends. Miriam walked ahead of her and the crowd. We stayed right there close to her every step of the way. Raymond was the one that saw it coming. Delores took a running start, and jumped on Miriam's back, and brought her to her knees! She went down on the sidewalk, and all we could see was blood where her knee cap was supposed to be! She shouldn't have done that. Miriam flipped that big ox of a girl off of her, and tried to get up and walk away, again! Raymond grabbed Miriam's right arm to help her walk. Delores had the whole crowd laughing at this point. She tried to sneak Miriam again. This time, didn't go like the last. Malcolm saw her coming at Miriam. He put his leg out, tripped her big butt, and yelled "Miriam, come get yo RESPECT!" Miriam doubled back, straddle Delores with her bad leg stretched out to the side, and she went to work on her! We didn't see where or when the pencil got in Miriam's hand. All we knew was, Delores' face looked like an etch-a-sketch board! We thought that Miriam had lost her mind the way she wearing Delores out!

In the projects, everyone understood the "Respect Factor". Miriam was walking along, minding her business, and Delores messed with her on the way to school, and on the way back home. Miriam walked away both times. As much as Raymond liked a good humbug, he didn't even try to push Miriam to go ahead and put Delores in her place. One thing we all knew was this; Miriam wouldn't start a fight, but, she didn't mind finishing one when provoked. We knew that the words that Delores said were hurtful to Miriam, because they were hurtful to us! Whatever the words were that broke Miriam's ability to hold her peace and keep her cool about all the stuff Delores was bluffing her with…was a mystery to everybody. When Miriam felt her bloody knee dripping blood down to her new Penny loafers, and her new Bobby socks, was what I believed it took. She had actually tried to get up and limp away.

One thing Miriam knew for sure was, she couldn't go back home and tell Jazzy that she didn't try to fight back! She learned that when she let the bi-racial girl that moved in across the street from us push her around.

For some reason, Miriam thought that she wasn't supposed to hit this girl back! She would let her pull her bows out of her head, throw dirt on her, and all sorts of mean things! Then one day she messed around and spit on Miriam. Miriam came home crying. Jazzy made Miriam wash her face, and stood by the door and waited for her to come back down the hall to her. She told Miriam, "You do know that you are going right back over there and you gonna whip her for old and new right?" Miriam started to cry. Jazzy slapped her so quickly, she came to straight attention! Jazzy told her, "Now, You go your black ass back over there, and if you don't beat her ass real good…you are gonna have to take a whipping from her, and another ass whipping from me, when you get back here! Get on over there and let her and her mammy know, you don't spit on NO child of mine! Go knock on that door and call her little pale ass outside, and you better wear her out!" That's exactly what Miriam did. She was proud of herself, for herself! That fight, (or slaughter I should say) triggered something in Miriam. She didn't need much provoking from that point on.

I believe this thing with her being so slow about her fighting Delores was because she looked at her not only as friend, but like a sister. Jazzy knew we argued and fought at home, when we are with each other. But, she warned us that we better not EVER fight each other out in the streets among others! She believed, if you allowed other people to see you fight each other, they would feel that they could mistreat us as well, because, we wouldn't stick together.

Well, that day we stuck together. Malcolm and Raymond had Miriam by the arms, and me and Deginna and Sasha had her back! We walked home with our heads held high. Delores was left there on the ground, with the others looking at her in disbelief. How could she have talked all of that crap and got beat up so badly?

When we finally got home, Jazzy was startled to see the blood that ran down Miriam's leg, and how she had all of the grass in her big, beautiful afro! She was franticly asking each of us what had happened. We all knew how much Raymond wanted to be the one to tell the story. He didn't just enjoy fighting, he loved to tell of who beat who in a good fight. So, we let him do all of the talking. He had to take our mama back to the point of us getting ready for school, and meeting up with him and Deginna nem. Jazzy told him, "Boy, just get to the damned point!" as she was fidgeting with the corner of her cigarette pack. By the time Raymond had gotten to the end of his version of the story, there was a big bam bam at the door!

Jazzy told me to go help Miriam get cleaned up and to get all of that grass out of her hair! Mama took pride in our hair, especially Miriam's. She had what we would call "Good Hair", it was jet black, thick and wavy, long hair. Even though we had Black Foot Indian from my grandmother's mama; we hated when the kids would say, "Y'all must got Indian in y'all blood, y'all hair too good to just be "Black folk hair."'! Jazzy told us not to entertain such foolishness. So; we would just walk away from any of them that did that.

We wanted to hang around the front of the house so we could see who was at the door. We headed down the hall, but lurked back far enough not to be seen, but close enough to hear what was being said. Miriam put all of her weight up against me as I was trying to squat and listen. I could hear Jazzy talking in that tone that she did when she was just about ready to fight! We eased a bit closer. The person she was talking to was the superintendent of the projects. Nobody liked him. He always acted like he owned the place. If he came to check on or inspect your apartment, he referred to everything as "My" this or "My" that. When our stove went out and had to be replaced, he came down when the maintenance guy was putting it in place of the other one. He goes, "Now, you gone need to be careful with my stove. I can't be buying appliances every time these folk break something." He knew full well that he wasn't paying for Jack around there! I don't even know why he was up in our house on this particular day? Well, I soon found out. Jazzy came strutting down the hall, and we couldn't move fast enough to even get to the bathroom. She didn't say nothing. She just grabbed Miriam by the arm and told her, "Come on back up here and let me show this fool your knee." She was practically dragging her down the hall, because I was trotting trying to follow them. Mr. Hodges' jaw dropped when he laid his eyes on Miriam's head, then, his eyes trailed down to her knee and all of the drying blood all over her leg, sock and shoe! Jazzy, stood there with her hand on her hip, propped up with her cigarette, her head lifted high, taking a long draw on her cigarette. She blew the smoke out, for as long as it took for her to draw it in. I think she did it more as a bragging right, because he didn't believe Jazzy's story about the damage that was done to Miriam. Margarette, Delores' mom had given him her version of what happened. She wasn't even there! She had taken Delores to the emergency room at the Charity hospital. She sent Mr. Hodges over to have Miriam brought up on charges for mutilating Delores' face. Jazzy told him, "Now, you see how that Heffa done tore up Miriam's knee? Hell, my child can barely walk!" I'm waiting right now for Nadine to come take us to the Charity! My child was minding her own business. She tried to avoid whipping that cow's ass. But noooo, she couldn't leave it alone. She had to show off for her so called friends by making fun of me because I'm pregnant and I still got it!" She rolled her hips and popped her fingers and stuck her mouth out in a pouting position, and walled her eyes at Mr. Hodges. We all busted out at the seams laughing at her. All of us laughed except Malcolm that is. He was still having trouble with the idea of a man getting his mama pregnant. I wondered, did he realize how he came to be?

Chapter 14

One Sad Christmas Indeed

Despite all of the Eggnog and Christmas corals that decked the halls at our house, we were still mourning JoJo. It looked like every time L.B. came around, he would have to rehearse the times he and JoJo did this, and that. It would make us all cry with him! Peter would try to talk to the MAN in L.B. so he could try to be a bit stronger about things when he was among the women. That didn't do a bit of good! He cried more than the women! Nadine had had one too many and told him, "L.B., now we loved JoJo too. You ain't the only one that was his friend. But, you cry so much…hell, you don't even give me or the angels time to get a good cry out for him! Now hush!" All of us bust out laughing in unison! He couldn't help but to laugh too.

Days of icy streets and cloudy skies started to look like the norm around our town. Veronica and Jessica were spending the holidays with us. Peter worked long hours then. The times he was gone so long left mama somewhat cranky. She tried to get us to bear with her. She said that the morning sickness (as they call it) was taking so much out of her! I was full of questions about pregnancy, how it happened, how did a baby make someone have heartburn, by the amount of hair it had or not have? There were days that mama threw up as soon as she ate her food! She always wanted the ice that grew on side of the freezer walls! She would yell to Miriam, "Scrape me some ice in nair." It looked like that was all she could keep down!

I knew this time with Veronica nem being with us was too good to be true. You could tell when they had been around their mother when she was being conniving. Veronica would always try to ease up to mama to find out what her plans were for the Christmas shopping that she would be doing. She "needed" to know what they planned on telling Santa Clause her and Jessica wanted for Christmas. Mama always said, you can tell when grownups have been talking mess in front of their children about you, by the way the children treat you from the last time they saw you. That proved to be so true! When Veronica's mama learned that Jazzy was pregnant by Peter, she made a point to send her girls to our house as raggedy looking as possible. The stuff mama had made for them never made it back to our house! She would send them empty handed, not even with their own underwear! Mama said that that was some old games she called herself playing! That meant that they would have to shop for new clothes for them while they were with us. Peter was such a REAL MAN! After their mom pulled this stunt for the third time, Peter didn't take them back home. He had Jazzy take them right back home! He told her to pull up, blow the horn, and when anyone stuck their head out of the door, put them out and drive off! Yes, they cried. Yes Jazzy did too. But, Peter was determined to beat her at her game!

Jazzy made herself sick trying to plead with Peter to go back and get them after he got off work. I had never heard Peter raise his voice at anyone, except when they didn't call him when all of the commotion took place at the Social, and Jazzy had to be taken to the hospital. Jazzy wouldn't stop pleading with him, because he kept saying, "Just leave it alone Jazzy. Stop all of this unnecessary crying! You're making yourself sick for nothing! I'm not about to go over there to get them! Etta is gonna have to learn to stop fu…Look Jazzy, Just leave it alone! I didn't come home to have to go through this bullshit! She has pulled this for the last time! I'm not going and you not going over there either! When she thinks about how she is messing up things for the girls, and not for me and you…she will soon give up, and act like somebody with some sense because; I'm here to stay. I'm in this for the long haul! She can give it up now! If she don't want to cooperate with us, I'll just keep being happy with our kids here, and the one that's coming! Now, you go in there and wash your face and let this go. Between JoJo and Miriam's leg being all busted up, and L.B. crying every other day…I've had enough Jazzy! I plan on having the best Christmas I've had in a long time. Etta is not gonna mess this one up, not this time! Gone in there and wash your face Jazzy, gone now!"

Me and Sasha just watched in awe! We were so moved when Peter said that he would just be happy to be with his kids here, and the one on the way! We were just standing there kinda hugging each other and didn't even realize it! You have to understand, me and Sasha fought every night when we slept in the same bed! If I touched her foot, accidently mind you. Or, if she pulled the cover off of me…accidently, we had to fight! So, to be standing there with her holding each other was a miracle of the season! When we realized it, we just eased away from each other and put a few feet between us. Mama just moped as she passed us and went to the bathroom to freshen up, and Peter sat at the foot of the bed to take his work boots off. He told us to stop looking at him with the puppy dog eyes, because he was not going to get the girls. We just hung our heads and left out of the room. We didn't want to mess up nothing for us, by pouting over Veronica and Jessica.

I rather enjoyed when we had Peter to ourselves. It felt like I had my own daddy for a while. I liked to hang out by the car with him when he would tune it up, or repair something on it. He was never impatient with the many questions I had. I actually learned the names, and how to identify the various tools he used because, he would ask me to pass them to him by their names. He challenged me to learn the parts of the car, and to be prepared to tell them when he touched them by memory the next time he raised the hood. That was the times when I felt like one of the boys. He made his buddies "watch their mouths" if they cussed while I was out there under the hood with him. I would just about be in stitches laughing on the inside, because, there was always that one that would swell up and try to mouth off at Peter for having me out there with grown folk anyway! He'd just tell them, "If you got a problem with it, you can carry the Hell on away from here." He didn't raise his voice, he just told them with that dry tone he spoke so slowly with. I would brag to Malcolm about how much more I knew about cars than him. He would always just say, "Do I really look like I care?" Then he would answer his own question, "No, I don't do I?" I hated when he did me like that!

Jazzy had begun going out with Peter to "Christmas Parties" and would always come back with gifts that stayed wrapped up from their friends that always told them to wait until Christmas day to open them. I thought, they must have some really nice friends that Peter knew. Because, none of Jazzy's friends ever did that before she met Peter.

They went to so many "Christmas Parties" that there were gifts for them all over the living room floor by Christmas Eve!

Miriam and Patsy were busy helping with the cooking. Nadine and Jazzy got together and hit the stores and came back to close up in Jazzy's room to wrap gifts that they said were for the grownups in their life. Somehow; that seemed like a little fib in my thinking. But, you don't question, or call an adult a fibber.

Sasha made a point to ease an occasion on the table to ask when Veronica nem would be coming since it's so close to Santa Clause coming. Peter was calm and had a strong determined look on his face all evening. As the night got under way, and the cakes were all finished, and Charles Brown had sung, "Please come home for Christmas" for the umpteenth time, I sadly went down the hall to get my bath, and to go to bed. It was not the Christmas that I had hoped it would be. I thought we would be in the kitchen helping mama cook like we did at Thanksgiving. This was not happening. Peter stuck to his guns about teaching Ella a lesson about using his girls as "game pieces"! He didn't pick them up, and didn't allow Jazzy to bring them over there! I didn't know he meant for Christmas too!

I crawled up into Miriam's bed, because you could see down the hall from her bed. I was so hopeful that my wish for Santa to get them to change their minds and I would see Veronica and Jessica come running down the hall to find me and Sasha. It didn't happen like that. I just couldn't get to sleep! Everyone had gone to their houses, the lights were out, and Miriam had come to her bed, and gave me the lecture about getting up and going to the bathroom on time. I flipped and flopped to the point that Miriam put me out of her bed! I didn't want to wake Sasha up and have her grumpiness to cause us to get a late night sleeping pill, with Peter's belt and end up missing Santa Clause's visit to our house!

So, I eased in the bed, and slipped under the covers, being careful not to pull too much cover from her. Good. Now to just get some sleep!

Santa Clause was so real to me, that, in my mind, I could hear the sleigh bells ringing as he shook the reins to make the reindeers go faster. I could actually hear the hoofs of the reindeers trampling on the roof top! Really, I did! I would close my eyes really tight to make sure that Santa wouldn't see me awake and put ashes in my eyes!

Morning couldn't come fast enough! I had an excitement, yet; a sadness that I couldn't quite explain. I didn't know if it was more about Veronica and Jessica not being there, or me not being at the Tyler's. I knew how much Mrs. Tyler wanted me there to share our first Christmas together. But, why wasn't any effort made to have me over there? I kinda felt like the thing that I was trying to keep from telling mama about what Mrs. Tyler had said about her and Peter's living together, had already been discussed between them. Neither one of them mentioned me going to spend the holiday where. When my Thanksgiving time was spent with mama nem, I was for sure we had mentioned me spending Christmas with the Tylers. She never even called me to ask me what I wanted to do! She nor Jeremy and Robbie didn't even call me! I tried to act as if all of the toys that Santa Clause had brought us was making me happy, especially the pretty sapphire blue bicycle that mama said was sent by Mrs. Tyler from Santa Clause. What kind of mess was that?! She could have Santa bring me a beautiful bike, but, none of them could call me to see why I wasn't coming over there! I was really trying to have a merry Christmas.

The morning started off with the Love story of how the virgin Mary had gave birth to baby Jesus, and how a man named Simeon said he could go ahead and die in peace because, he had finally saw the savior of the world! You know the story in the book of St. Luke. Mama read that to us and told us for as long as I could remember, that Jesus was the reason we celebrate Christmas! We weren't allowed to even open one gift in the house until we had heard the reading of the story of the birth of our Lord! It was tradition, and a serious thing to mama for us to never forget Jesus! That was the only thing that felt RIGHT about that morning!

Sasha had to give me attitude about MY new bike! She wanted to know why I was the only one that got a shiny new bicycle like I was all special or something! Mama just told her, "The morning is going just fine without you starting mess!" Sasha was fine with my having a new shiny bike, as long as I let her try to ride it as long as she wanted. When Malcolm got tired of trying to help her stay UP, she had to have something to raise hell about! For her to be so little, and sickly, she was a firecracker! Raymond loved that about her! He would do stuff to egg her on! She didn't mind it one bit either! She stayed ready to accommodate his wishes. There was a little black…I mean Black girl in the neighborhood that tried to befriend Sasha. She came over to our block every evening that she could to try to bring treats or tokens of some sort to show her good intentions toward Sasha. Instead of taking her acts of kindness for just that, Sasha would make her stand outside of the back door, snatch her treats or toys she brought over, and slam the door in her face! We knew just who it was when we heard the door slam. Me and Malcolm would just shake our heads and keep doing whatever we were doing. But, Raymond would coach Sasha on how to get her little friend back over there so she could get something else out of her! When mama found out how she was doing the little girl, she told her mama to keep her from over there because, Sasha was not gonna break her window out of her door frame, being ridiculous towards her daughter! The lady told mama, she needed to teach Sasha some manners! That didn't go over too well.

After all of the paper clutter from opening gifts was over, we had breakfast, and I had to know why the Tylers were not mentioned past the bike, and not much before the bike coming there! Mama just muttered under her breath, "I'm gonna let her tell you why." I knew what that look meant. She had indeed had words with Mrs. Tyler about Something!

Despite all of the gifts and food and desserts, the turkey just kinda chewed to the corner of my mouth and set up a ball in my jaw. It was hard to follow through and bring myself to just swallow it! Sasha was still being as ornery as ever. Miriam was more than pleased with all of the stuff she had gotten for Christmas. So was Malcolm. Miriam had gotten the creepy looking Chatty Cathy doll that she wanted. Why she wanted her, I don't know. She was spooky looking to me, and, she sounded like she was cussing or something when she would whisper her secret to you! Malcolm got all kinds of stuff! A new football, G.I. Joe stuff, Lincoln Logs, cowboy gear to wear, a live sounding machine gun, you name it, it was bound to be coming from under the tree! Miriam had gobbled her food down and put on her new clothes and Go-go boots and coat and went over to show Patsy her new doll and outfit. Malcolm kept going over to tell Peter and mama thank you. Sasha yelled at him, "You need to be telling Santa Clause thank you ole crazy boy!" Peter looked at Malcolm and gave him a wink and said, "That's right boy, you thank Santa Clause!"

We ate and cleared the table. I wanted to hang close by Peter and Jazzy to see if they were going to bring up going to get Veronica and Jessica at some point that day. Peter didn't bulge. Jazzy had a sick spell again. So, she went to her room after coming out of the bathroom. I asked Peter who all of the other gifts were for that were still under the tree? He said that they were for his other girls whenever they came back over. He called them, his "other girls"! That really did something for me! That meant we were his girls too! I asked Sasha did she hear what Peter said. She said real dry like, "I'm sitting right here ain't I?" I could have smacked her! She was a terror when she wanted to be!

Peter was a man of strong convictions about keeping his word. He said he was gonna teach Etta a lesson, and that's what he did. He was also trying to teach Veronica something too. I heard him telling mama that Veronica was getting to be just as devious as her mama! He had to show her that it was gonna cost her to play the snoop and the snitch for her low down mammy! It also cost me to have a more pitiful day than I ever would have expected! I really enjoyed playing with Veronica and Jessica. Veronica had such a wild and busy imagination! She could think of all kinds of games to play that kept our times together so much fun!

Peter's punishment had a good and a bad outcome. The good was that, it showed Etta that she was not going to run nothing over at Jazzy's house! But; it caused all of the children to miss their Christmas holiday together! He said that Veronica was gonna learn a lesson, that came at the expense of Jessica missing out! But, before the sun went down on Christmas day, he left the house, with slumped shoulders, and didn't say a word to none of us! He just got the keys and left! Mama, tried to keep the cool, and calm way that she usually had about herself. The thing that my nosey intuition always got me in trouble with Jazzy about is this: I got this thing from the Lord I know. But, I didn't know, it wasn't a nosey problem…it was called discernment. I always allowed it to cause me to have to act upon everything I was able to see, instead of, watching, and waiting for the person's next move! I didn't know how to be led by the Spirit of the Lord at that age. I was not even sure that mama had seen that gifting of God in me at that age yet. I had to let mama know that I knew something was up with Peter, and I needed to know what she thought it might be. She just kept on messing around in the kitchen, humming and wiping down stuff that she had already wiped before. I had to remind her of that too. She politely told me, "Take your frail tail in there, and stay in a child's place. Peter didn't ask you for permission to go nowhere did he?" I said, "No but," she cut me off again. "If he needed your permission or input, he would have asked you for it. Now, go sit down somewhere." I knew that meant for me to hush too!

Before long, I heard Peter's car come up. I felt relieved. I didn't want him to have been upset and to have left us because of it. I tried to act calm and stay put until he came through the door, but, I couldn't because I heard a sound that couldn't be mistaken for any other sound. It was a piercing cry of JESSICA! She had slammed her finger in the car door! We all got up and ran to see what the matter was. When she saw mama, she ran smack into her belly and hugged her so tight that mama had to tell Peter to pry her off of her because she was hurting her stomach! Get this, Veronica ran to hug Sasha! You know this had to be a weird Christmas! Malcolm even had a big grin on his face! This called for some more eating and gift opening for them!

Veronica had asked Santa to bring her the Chrissy doll that had a button you push in her stomach and it made her hair grow out of the top of her head! It grew all down her back! And she was a kinda tall doll! There were clothes, games toys, shoes, coloring books, water paints,

Eazy Bake ovens for me and Sasha, and one for Veronica and Jessica to take home! I knew Peter was a good man! Not because of all of the stuff he told Santa to bring us. But, because he didn't leave Veronica and Jessica to agonize over not spending Christmas with him and us! I believe Jessica would have just been pleased to see Jazzy and eat some of her good cooking! She really loved being with mama so much, I believe that is why God allowed mama to get pregnant with Peter's baby.

In all that was done that Christmas, I learned the joy of it was this: Jesus, family, giving of ourselves to see someone else happy. That's exactly what Jesus came for.

Now, to get to the bottom of why the Tylers didn't try to see me for Christmas! Didn't call me or NOTHING!

Chapter 15

In ALL Things; He knows

The Tylers were a morally sound family. They were a giving family. Whether because of compassion for Jazzy's cramped life or her desire for a daughter of her own; Mrs. Tyler wanted me in her life. At least I thought she did. The way my mama said that she would let her tell me why I wasn't asked over for Christmas, let me know there was something going on. I waited until everyone in the house was distracted and on to enjoying their gifts before I slipped into mama's room to call the Tylers. Robbie answered the phone. At first he was excited to hear my voice. Then, Mrs. Tyler asked who was on the phone. He covered the mouth piece. When he returned, he was not the same excited to hear my voice guy. Just like mama said, "You can tell when parents have said negative things around their kids." I could see if it was Jeremy that had switched on me that fast. But, Robbie! This was hard on me. Robbie was loyal to me when no one else was! I asked him what his mom said to him. He just dryly said, "We can't be family with you anymore." I dropped the phone! That same frozen that I experienced with the military guy, was the frozen that I got when Robbie said those words to me! I was sick! All I could do was scream "mamaaaa!" She came running, and so did Peter. She started twisting me and searching for damage all over my body! I just shook loss from her and started crying and breaking down! Peter reached out and pulled me to himself, and hugged me and patted my head like I was a new puppy or something! I shook away from him. I guess my spirit was trying to reject him before he rejected me too! Mama saw the phone on the floor. She asked who I had been talking to. I was struggling to get his name out. When she realized I was trying to say, Robbie, she slammed the phone down, sat me down on the bed, and asked me what he said to me. When I could finally tell her, she was pissed off in the worst way! She picked up the phone and dialed the Tyler's house again. Mrs. Tyler answered the telephone. 'Jazzy's came to the forefront of the conversation at this point. Mama took a seat on the sideline for a moment. Jazzy said, "When you got on your throne to put your mouth on my relationship to Peter; that was one thing. But; when you mess with my child, you know you have gone too damn far! No! I listened to you put me down and condemn me to Hell. Now, you're gonna hear me out! As long as I was catering to your wishes and allowing Monia to come and go with you as you pleased, that was fine. You did very nice things for her. I was the BEST person on the planet, as long as I let you have my child for your desires to be fulfilled. I had compassion on you, while you thought I was pitiful. You have what looks like the perfect life, a beautiful home, a nice career, a picture perfect family. But, all the while, you are lonely and empty. When you asked me to give you an opportunity to "HELP" me with my load, I saw right through you, and I began to pray and ask the Lord to help YOU with the burden that you carry! Here's the thing you failed to realize; my house was filled with LOVE! My sisters and my friends all piled up over my house because, they felt loved when they were there. Dummy, and the punks (as you called them) and all of the rift raft and Misfits that you referred to them as, knew they were loved and not JUDGED when they came to my house. When Monia came to your house, and things got difficult for her to deal with, or she needed understanding about the things that went on over YOUR house, she called ME! When you realized, despite all of the gifts, and monetary tokens that you tried to use to win her heart from me were all in vain, you sent your boys on a special mission over here to spy out what makes MY HOUSE so special. Let me guess... they told you they were made to feel like they were family too? Look, I'm not gonna put your womanhood down because you can't give your husband no more children. Because, one thing I know, it's the Lord that opens the womb. You have to take that up with Him. As for Monia, I was blessed when He gave her to me. Every last one of them are my blessings from Him. So, I'm just gonna remember the good things you did for her. I chose not to acknowledge the fact that you tried to use her as a pawn in your game, to manipulate your husband into paying money for you to get anymore medical procedures that could possibly help you to have another child. That (mind you) wasn't even sure to be a girl baby anyway! Yes, I believe you loved Monia. I believe you would have adopted her and given her the world. But, I can't help it if your hang-ups with your husband and you being angry with him, AND God have you so bitter! You are NOT going to take it out on my child! She is a very discerning little girl, and she's suffered in silence even to this day! I'll be damned if I'll let it go another day further! You know you could've called her and at least said Merry Christmas or something! Stuff don't mean nothing to her if she can't feel the heart behind it! Any judgment you have for me and Peter, you take that up with God too. I know in my heart, I have shown you love. That is ALL I owe you! You, don't have no friends now because, you don't know what real love is! You love with a self-serving agenda. God's love reaches outward to others. You give to get praise from man, Love gives looking for nothing in return. I might live in the projects, but, I have a home of love. Now, I don't know how you plan to fix this with Monia, I don't know if this was your way of easing out of her life because, you don't agree with how I'm living mine. But, I do know you owe her an answer. You can't sashay into her life and give her a pie in the sky dream of a life with her "brothers" and, everything she could ever dream of having, when you knew from the beginning that your husband wasn't for all of that! While you're judging my life, you need to get on your knees and ask the Lord to clean you up! Hell, I know I ain't all I could be! I have to ask the Lord for forgiveness daily for something! One thing I do know is this, I am striving to keep my relationship with the Lord until I die! I am striving to love his people like He told me to, you included. Now, if I don't measure up to your standard of what you think I should be living for the Lord, then, you pray for me! Don't you dare take it out on my child! Peter and I will be parents to a child that was conceived in love. Peter and I will be married one day soon. I know you don't understand how this could all be, and, I don't care to be explaining my business to you and no other woman. But, do know this; I have made my peace with the Lord about what I'm doing over here in New Roads. I suggest you do the same about what goes on over there at your house." She didn't slam the phone down like before. She placed it in the cradle like she usually did when she had had a good conversation with Peter or one of her friends. Then she hugged me and told me, "You got all the love you need over here with this family baby."

Some of the things I heard Jazzy say about Mrs. Tyler not being able to have any more children, and being bitter with God hurt me inside. But, some of it made me see a lot of things that a little girl shouldn't be able to understand at that time in life. But, I did. I knew that LOVE is what was making all of this stuff work. I knew that the Lord looked at our way of doing things through eyes of love and patience with us. I felt bad that she told Mrs. Tyler that I would sneak in calls to her when I didn't feel ok about things that went on in her house. I felt it would make her feel that she was not being a good enough mother to me. That's what she wanted the most, to be a mother to a DAUGHTER.

I wanted the love at this house to be enough for me. But, me needing understanding about the things that had happened to the people in our lives that were no longer there because, death, murder, betrayal, now this with the Tylers left me feeling dismayed and very sad. I wanted to believe love was gonna be enough. But, I needed some questions answered! I asked mama if I could talk to her in the room with just me and her. She just gave Peter a look and he left the room and closed the door behind him. Mama sat on the bed, and patted the spot on side of her for me to take a seat. I did. She asked me, "What's going on in that pretty head of yours 'Henny'?" I asked her with tears in my eyes, "Mama, why don't nobody know what happened to JoJo? It seems like they are not trying to find out any more either. It almost seems like he didn't matter to people because he was a sissy! She corrected me. "He was different from other men." Well why did they just put him in the ground and everybody went home and never tried to find out who did that to him. And, and, what about Dave, he was always so sad? Why he don't come around no more. He really needed friends in his life. Nadine is always grumpy and fussing, but, she has friends and people always want her around! But, nobody wants Dave around. I don't understand. And, Mrs. Tyler has all of the things that a little girl could want. But, she can't even have a little girl! That military guy, where is he? Why he don't never come back to see you? Mama, why don't Malcolm ever act happy?

Delores thinks something is wrong with you for having a baby, and babies are beautiful! What is wrong with her?! Why do I keep having all of these bad dreams at night, and you say monsters aren't real? Mama, why do we live in a place where white folks don't want to come to, and the only ones in this town are the two that take money from us, and want us out of their store real quick! Why are we, always the ones that seem like so much is wrong with us because we live in the projects?! This don't feel like no ***love*** mama!" At that point I just collapsed on mama's lap sobbing and exhausted in my little soul! Mama didn't know what to say for a long time. Then, she said something that I would never forget. She said, "Baby, sometimes when y'all would go to bed at night, and everything is quiet, I find myself getting out of my bed, going into the kitchen to try to figure out what I would be able to feed y'all the next day. Then, I would walk down the hall and peep in the room on each of y'all with tears in my eyes because of the life that we were living at the time. I would go into the bathroom, and sit there so overwhelmed that I could not even find the words to say, after all of the words of comfort I had offered to everyone else. I would sit there as the tears rolled down my face and fell into my lap, and I knew all of the things that I wanted to say, all of the things I thought I needed for my life at that moment. But; all that I could muster was these words, "Lord, you know." And guess what I found out child? He KNEW! Somehow, someway, the food came, the bills got paid, the things that had been wrong, were made right. The people that were not good for my life were moved out of it, the lonely days were filled with laughter and something adventurous that y'all would do. Baby, for all of these question you have, and the reasons why things are as they are, our heavenly father knows all things, and he's gonna answer it all…by and by." Believe it or not, that was good enough for me.

Chapter 16

Wrong Motives, Wrong Outcomes

I never got a call from Mrs. Tyler over the time that we were out of school on the Christmas break. I never thought that I could face her again with the same admiration that I had for her when she was my first grade teacher. I guess I couldn't get past Robbie's words to me on the phone that late Christmas evening. I made every effort to avoid the walk to the cafeteria. Because, that meant that I would have to pass by Mrs. Tyler's class. She seemed to not need me anymore. The feeling left me with a stabbing sensation inside. My mouth felt clamped shut really tight. I was always that one that wanted to be needed. There! I admitted it. I was so sure that her needing me was going to be a lasting thing. I thought that it was my insurance of Robbie and Jeremy being in my future. Somehow, I thought that I would never get over the fantasy of Jeremy and I having a life together. Even as a child, I knew that there was a point of having to let go. I had the whole package of REJECTION, from the entire family! I was living in a state of so much emotion from the Tylers! I felt that Mr. Tyler threw me away long time ago! He wasn't accepting of things from the beginning. He was not too keen on things especially when he had to beat the breaks off of Jeremy when he learned that he and Robbie got into it about him having feelings for me. I still wanted him to father me. I felt like he would be the best replacement, at the time that I came into their lives for the "Military Guy". I was certain that he was the answer!

From the conversation that I overheard Jazzy having with Mrs. Tyler, it was pretty clear to see that, her and Mr. T had been having problems for a while! You would never know it! I think back now...he was rather uptight most times. He was a sort of, no nonsense kind of guy. That was still better than the feeling that I was left with from the "Military Guy".

I tried to get out of the cafeteria really fast too. The way the school was set up, you could see the auditorium stage from where we sat to have lunch. That only served to remind me of the night of the talent show. The night when Miriam nem stole the show! But, for that, JoJo lost his life.

There had been a lot of talk among the kids that were from the upper class about what, and who was the one that they needed to be looking at for his death. In all of the talk, (that I managed to always be privy to) there were some things that made a whole lot of sense to me.

Remember the big, quiet, really sinister guy that would come through the campus and through the hood from time to time? Well, his sister that was so hot tailed around the school with the different boys was one of the girls cozied up smooching with JoJo's brother! From what they said, she was only brushing up to him to get him to put in a plug for her to be picked as one of the dancers for Miriam's dance troop. JoJo saw right throw that mess! He didn't only see to her not being on the dance team, he had her reported to the Principal's office for being behind the building with some manish tail boy!

It was said that, because it wasn't JoJo's brother with her, that that was the reason he reported her. This caused his brother to jump on her and beat her up pretty badly. They said that Ole Dude wasn't about to let it be said that he would take revenge out on, "just a kid". So, he came after the one said to be responsible for her getting suspended from school, whipped by her mom, and jumped by his baby brother!

Some of the kids said that, that didn't make no sense. Because," Ole Dude didn't have to beat up no Punk!" They said that was too easy for him. I guess that they didn't know him like they thought they did. They came smack in the middle of the evening when you would least expect it! He was standing on the sideline watching us play football, (as it was his custom to do some evenings). He would stroll through the neighborhood, not saying anything to anybody. He would stand there looming over everybody. Because, he was sooo BIG compared to most of the people in the projects! He stood there with the toothpick hanging out the side of his mouth, not giving off any real expression. Most of the time you didn't know what he was thinking or feeling. He would give me that nod and wink of approval when he came through and saw me playing with the guys. It always let me know that he was saying. "You can do it. Don't let them make you think because, you a girl, you can't play just as good as these Scallywags out here!" That got me so pumped when he did that! He didn't do it that day though. He was almost looking past us it seemed. It was like a different day out there with the guys.

Out of nowhere, the cops came! Like 2 carloads of them! I believe they felt it would take that many of them to take him in! But, you know what? When they swarmed upon him, he didn't try to shake them off, or resist them at all! Not like someone that was innocent of killing my mama's dear friend, and my babysitter. He just put his hands out and allowed them to put the handcuffs on him. Back then, they put the cuffs on you in the front of you, instead of hands behind your back. I was just shocked! I just always believed that they had him pegged wrong! I thought he was just a gentle giant that everyone misunderstood. I was on the bottom of a pile up when they came for him. It was so weird! I just didn't want to accept this madness! I certainly wanted JoJo's killer brought down! I just didn't want it to be Ole dude! I looked at him with so much hurt and disappointment in my spirit! Why couldn't they get someone else?! I had so much respect for the 'Cool' in him. He commanded respect without a word out of his mouth! His presence demanded it!

You know, I thought it would give me closure and help me understand the mystery of what God was doing in letting JoJo get murdered by someone that used to take up for the underdogs in their hood. That is why I admired him so much. I felt the same way. But, that made no sense to me or Big Mama.

Chapter 17

Running Won't Fix It Monia

Jazzy was busy making herself another maternity dress. She didn't like for us to disturb her while she was sewing. So, I eased into to room, and patted her on the shoulder. Without looking back, she said, "What is it Monia?" I just blurted out, "Mama how is God supposed to be pleased, (or as the grown folk said, Get His glory out of) when "Dummy died wrong, and JoJo died wrong, and, and now, "Ole Dude locked up for the rest of his life...and Mrs. Tyler can't have any more babies and mad at you because you can, and all of this bad and crazy stuff is happening all of the time in the Projects! Why is it so bad and hard to have a happy life here all of the time mama?! She let me say everything I had to say. Well, yell. Then, she turned around in her seat. She reached to put both of her hands on both of my shoulders. I jerked back and took out running out of the front door! I knew when she did like that, she was about to start explaining why God "moved" in certain ways. I asked the "God question". But, I really guess I didn't want to hear the "God answer". I was running and crying. Didn't know where I was running to. I just needed to run until I could get away from that place. That place where too much was going wrong and too much hurting was happening to some really good people that I just happened to care about! I didn't look for "Dummy", he came to my window and found me. I didn't ask for JoJo to be my babysitter. He just ended up there and Jazzy took him and L.B. in. Mrs. Tyler didn't get to pick which students would be hers. I just ended up being put in her class. So, what was God really doing?! I didn't see any good in what He was doing! I just realized, I was down there by "that church". Where Jazzy went to deal with those "church goers", that threw bottles at "Dummy" and cut him on his already chopped off thumb...that ended up being the death of him! I did a quick spin on a dime! I didn't want to be nowhere near no church or no phony church folk! Bam! I ran smack into the new boy, Gill! "What you following me for?" "Monia yo mama looking for you!" I started running like he was after me on the football field! I ran harder as he got closer! By the time I was back by my house, Jazzy was in the doorway yelling, "Stay with her!" I ran in the direction of Ms. Rosa's store. She was out there with a broom, sweeping nothing! She was trying to see what the kids "over there" on the bad end of the Projects was up to now. This end was where the "Bullies" lived. The end we lived on was considered where the "Underdogs" lived. You couldn't get Jazzy to agree with that nonsense! She always told us in 49A that we were supposed to look out for the underdogs in the world.

I was running so fast, all I could see was Ms. Rosa looking like she was moving in slow motion. It was like; she was trying to wave her arms like the guys when they are flagging the cars to slow down for the final lap of the race. Before I could make out her words, all I heard was, SCREEEECHHHH! I felt Gill snatch me up by the back of my shirt so hard it spun me around, and over the other side of his back! I saw Jazzy holding the bottom of her belly trying to hobble down the sidewalk as best as she could without putting her other child in danger. I saw the terror in her eyes. I looked around Gill to see what had terrified Jazzy. I saw a few cars halted in the street, a big burly, red faced white man yelling cuss words in my direction! I heard him say the forbidden 'N' word! Gill dropped me! Ms. Rosa came from her direction with the broom in the air towards the big monster looking man. Gill was crossing the street to come at him too. Horns were blowing; people were shaking their fist out the window at the man. Jazzy had finally hobbled her way to where I was, fell upon me out of breath, and was squeezing the wind out of me! Then, I realized that I was about to run into oncoming traffic! The "Monster" was cussing and growling because, he barely missed hitting me! This explained why Jazzy was trying to get to me and risked herself to try to save me! I froze in my mind for a brief moment. It made me think about what the preacher had said about what Jesus had sacrificed to die for us! This was something that captured my attention just for that moment. I was soon back onto this dude trying to cuss out a child. I was laughing so hard! Ms. Rosa was whopping that big man so hard with that "Nosy broom"! Even the other people in the cars were laughing at her. Jazzy had to sit on Ms. Rosa's steps and recollect herself. She was trying to keep from laughing so hard! She knew that she needed every breath to keep that baby in her!

I soon put my wall back up. Gill was still standing there at the car of the big man. I rolled my eyes at him, instead of thanking him for saving my life. Gill started towards me with a genuinely heartfelt smile on his face. I took off running again. The “over there” was what Ms. Rosa was dry sweeping and gazing upon. That's where we were forbidden to go to. Well, I didn't care. I was not trying to be nowhere near Jazzy, and I didn't want to be where they were doing or saying “God stuff”! I ran over on to the “Stomping Ground” of the “Bullies”. That's what we called the places where we got down, where we fought, where I was shocked when I went running through there! All of the people that Ole Dude had led the gang fights to protect, were laughing, drinking, and acting a fool! They were acting just as if he was still there and not locked up, for possibly the rest of his life! How could this be so? How could they be drinking, turning up their beer and wine bottles while Ole Dude was in jail, waiting to be sent to trial and sentenced for murdering someone that, L.B., and a few others did not believe that he had done! These clowns were partying like they were celebrating the fact that he was locked up, like he was their enemy! As I was running, I got madder and madder. I started running harder. Then, I saw Janice running towards me. She was Miriam's age. Janice was the one in the corners of the auditorium, with this guy or the other at the socials. She didn't have any business with me. I'm just an 8 year old little girl that had done nothing to her. So, why was she running towards me with fire in her eyes? Well, my mind was working like a whirlwind! The only thing that came to me was, “Drop down, and roll for their knees!” Malcolm taught me to do that in our football practice time. When she got about 3 feet away, I did just what he had taught me! She went flying into the air. I rose up, and started running some more. I heard one of the girls, I didn't see who. But, she yelled out, “You done messed up now little girl! She is pregnant!" I halted, looked back and saw them helping her up from the ground. I took off again!

Peter had been called at work to come get Jazzy and take her home. Ms. Rosa was trying to keep her from getting too close to the big man that was trying to explain to Ms. Rosa why he was so upset that he had called me a, well...the "N" word. She sent him on his way before Jazzy had the time to recollect her strength. I think that he had better leave more before Peter had gotten there! He was a quiet storm for real! He had set things in order with Jazzy, and gone back to work when he knew she was okay. She was in the back of the house by the time that I came down from my tree to see what Gill had heard when I left them back at the other end of the Projects.

He had to first jump up in my face to tell me that I need to "Stop acting a fool!" I shoved him back and told him, "Just tell me what happened after I left boy!" He had to know what had started me to crying in the first place. I didn't want him to know my business! That's why I was in my tree when I got back in the first place! He tried to tell me about them gathering up a crowd to come down here and get Janice's "Respect"! I told him, "If they didn't even care about Ole Dude getting locked up for life, and was out there dranking and getting their heads bad, (as Nadine called it) what did they care about Janice? He told me that I better get in there and tell Jazzy what was about to happen. I didn't believe it was about to go down, so, I didn't tell Jazzy nothing. I went in the house without telling him anything! I wasn't talking to someone that laughed at me when I fell! He was cute but, not cute enough to get my secrets. When I got inside, Sasha was sitting on the couch with her thumb in her mouth, rolling her eyes at me. To be so little and sickly, she always had a mouth full of something to say! "You done got Jazzy all upset and worried and she 'bout to bring this baby home early! You always doing stuff Monia!" I just rolled my eyes back at her, and told her to just sit over there and mind her own business. I wanted to be in the right place when Jazzy came from the back of the house. I knew she wasn't feeling too fond of me right now. So, I went over and sat by Sasha. She tried to kick at me to keep me from sitting too close to her. Same old song just a different day. She didn't want me sleeping close to her, and didn't want me to sit close to her either! She was just mean!

Jazzy came in the room and saw Gill still hanging around. "Boy, what you still doing here?" Gill looked at me to let me know that he was gonna tell it whether I liked it or not! “Ms. Jazzy, they say they getting the gang all together to come down here and beat yo baby outta you, because Monia hurt Janice and might make her lose her baby! Monia didn't even know she was gonna have no baby!” Jazzy looked at him, came closer and put her hand on her hip and asked him, “What the, who the hell said what?” Gill told her again what they said. She got her cigarettes, (back then no one said not to smoke while pregnant) got the telephone and called Nadine, Patsy, and L.B., and told them to “bring their shit and get over there right away.” They knew exactly what she meant! She gave Gill instructions to go down to the football field and get Malcolm, Bernard, and Raymond. “And run like you did after Monia!” He just laughed and darted out of the back door. She looked at me and said, “You see what yo little frail ass done got started?!” Sasha rolled her eyes at me again, took her waterlogged thumb out of her mouth and said, “See, I told you.” Jazzy yelled at Sasha, “You just sit there and hush! And take that nasty thing out of your mouth, and go over to Margarette, tell her, Miriam and Delores to get over here, Now!” Sasha drug her ornery feet as slow as she felt like going. She could not care less one way or, the other if they came or not. When she was in her own world with her thumb, she didn't want to be disturbed! She was just like an old woman sometimes! She didn't want the music too loud, or anybody having too much fun in a loud way around her. She was just mean!

Patsy was there with her Brass knuckles shined up. She had her “Peace maker” at her side. L.B., well, he had his dead daddy's old rusty machete, and his shot gun. He kept opening and checking to see if he was loaded up. Jazzy told him, “Boy, if you open that gun up one more time!” She never finished what she intended to say when she would do that. I guess he knew what the rest of the sentence would end like. Because, he never opened that gun back up. Everybody came over as asked to. Well, (was ordered to). Except, guess who? Nadine. That's right. She never came or did anything according to the rules! L.B. thought she was already over at Jazzy’s. Jazzy thought she was with him!

"Monia, call yo auntee and find out where she got her tail at!" I ran to the phone! I figured the "Bullies were really gonna do what they said they were gonna do by now. We needed all of the help we could get! Bernard was itching for a hum bug! Raymond was not really a fighter. He would go along with whatever came down the pike though. Malcolm didn't say much about what he would or could do. He just kept his cool, stayed mean, and did whatever he had to do in the hood

I was getting really nervous waiting for Nadine to answer the phone! It just rang, and rang! I knew that her big mouth alone was enough to scare off a few of the hoodlums anyways. "Why wouldn't she just answer the phone?" The front door was left open as we all filed out of the back door to the crowd that was ready to rumble with us. I was afraid to hang up and have to go back out and, have to tell Jazzy that I just didn't let the phone ring just "one more time"! I stood there twitching from side to side trying to hold my pee. I just couldn't hang the phone up! We needed Nadine's manpower! The twitching had turned into the squatting down to really hold it! All of a sudden, I get a bop on the back of my head! It made my pee go straight back up! "Hang that damn phone up and go pee with yo pissy tail!" Nadine! I hated her sometimes! I couldn't get an answer on the phone, because, she was there! Beating me upside my head! As I ran down the hall...I was like, "I hate you Nadine!" Of course, I didn't let her hear me. She was the life of the party, the one that taught me the really funky stuff about people, especially boys. But, the memory of my birthday party was raised from the dead when she did me like this today of all days! I don't know if I hated her, more than I was mad at God, or which. I just know I had me a good cry when I got in the bathroom! That was very short lived because; there was a sudden commotion out back! I didn't take time to wash my hands, which was a cardinal sin in our house! I darted out the door and to my surprise, L.B., was standing toe to toe with one of the police officers going off about the loss of his best friend JoJo! He had been holding it in for long enough. He never fully grieved according to Big Mama. She said that she pitied the day that it would really hit him. Well; today was that day.

The officer had his hand on his piece and the other officer had his Billy club, repeatedly hitting the palm of his hand. They knew full well why he was going off! What they didn't expect was all that would come out of his mouth.

Remember how L.B. and Nadine were sitting out in the car smoking that "Shit"? Well, that's what Big Mama said it was. That was the day that they saw the same officer, in plain clothes, off duty, pushing Ole Dude out of the back door of their house with a gun pointed at his back! Well, I guess the high finally wore off. Reality had set back in. L.B. and Nadine were both very alert, and aware that the officer that they were standing face to face with right now, was indeed the officer that they saw on my birthday. The officer was talking some old stuff about having him confused with someone else. I lunged out to say something that I saw when Malcolm was helping me up from my fall, and proceeding to punch Gill in the face. Miriam grabbed me back and told me between her clinched teeth "Shut yo big mouth before you get yo throat cut for telling on a policeman!" I quickly weaved from her grip to get Jazzy's attention. I had to get out what I saw! It might help get Ole Dude out of jail!

All eyes were on L.B. as he made his story plain through his tears. The hush that came over the entire crowd of so called "gang bangers", was in part because, everyone knew the closeness of the relationship between JoJo and L.B. So, the silence was from big bullies dropping their bats and sticks and coke bottles, and brass knuckles, and "peacemakers". They were actually being sympathetic to L.B. And some were even shedding tears! Jazzy and Nadine were still in fight mode, (you know, if necessary).

Nadine didn't like the way the officers were handling L.B... She staggered straight up in the officer's face, with her beer smelling breath and all. She proceeded to tell him about the day in the car. Every ear was wide open to hear what was going to come out of her mouth....

Jazzy always told us, when grown folk are talking, we need to stay in a child's place! That meant, hush your mouth! But, what L.B. was trying to get out was not coming fast enough, or the right way for me or Nadine. I broke loose from Miriam and pushed my way to Jazzy. I pulled on her arm to bring her ear down to me. She resisted me because, she was trying to see what Nadine was gonna say. I insisted again by pulling her arm. She looked at me with warning and frustration at the same time.

But, when she saw the look of urgency in my eyes, she bent down as much as her belly would let her. I told her that Nadine didn't see what I saw when I was trying to show off my birthday suit from Mrs. Tyler. Jazzy raised her hand for everyone to be quiet so I could tell her what I saw.

Nadine was puffing hard and rolling her eyes at me. She said out right, "Listen up you lil Heffa, you ain't telling nobody NOTHING! I got the damn flo!" Jazzy gave Nadine that look that everybody that knew Jazzy knew it meant, "You don't mess with my children"! Nadine knew that, Jazzy being pregnant put her in a hard place for fighting. But, it certainly didn't stop her from wobbling over to Nadine and snatching her by her hair and holding her head in a crook, with one hand, and her fist drawn back with the other. She was just about to slam her when Peter came up through the crowd and grabbed her fist and loosed her clinched grip from Nadine's hair. "What the? Let me go!" Peter had the hardest time getting her grip off of her hair! "You gone mess around and have this baby too early acting a fool around here the way you been doing Jazzy! You can't be running after Monia and out here running a gang fight, and trying to whoop up on Nadine...when you know you pregnant! What is wrong with you Jazzy?!" She pushed Nadine's head away from her and shook herself loose from Peter. She said, "If you knew what this Whore tried to handle my child like..., "Whore?! You ain't got no room to be calling me NOTHING! You having another baby by this Tom, Dick, and Harry, like all the rest of them illegitimate Bastards you got! And you calling me a Whore?! You taught me everything I know about Whoring, you Bitch you!" Jazzy was running towards Nadine like she was a charging Bull! Peter and Miriam were running towards her too! You don't play the dozens and you certainly don't tell no mama that her children are "Illegitimate Bastards! Even if a couple of them were. Nadine knew she had gone too far with Jazzy. Peter was running to get a head start over Jazzy to keep her from fighting with Nadine for certain this time! He did manage to keep Jazzy off of her. But, Miriam by passed them both. Peter had mama in one arm, and was reaching for Miriam with the other arm. Oops, it was too late! Miriam was taught to respect her elders. We all were. But, something was not registering in her mind at the moment she heard the words out of Nadine's mouth. She had already had to fight Delores for picking on Jazzy because she was, (in Delores's mind,) too old to be having a baby. Before Peter could grab Miriam, that left hook that she delivered to Delores, went straight to Nadine's jaw! The crowd went crazy! They were cheering Miriam because; the majority of them couldn't stand Nadine. She had either cursed them out or disrespected their parents as well.

Miriam hit her so hard the police officer that she had the confrontation with was laughing so hard that he had no mind to even try to get the crowd or Miriam under control!

Peter and Jazzy were standing with a look of relief, and pride on their faces. Relief because, Miriam had saved Jazzy from having to fight while she was so pregnant! Pride because, she was glad to see that Miriam had such a big heart for her family that, she would stand up for her siblings as well as her mama against Whoever!

The bullies forgot all about the reason that brought them to Jazzy's back door. They were so taken by the "Togetherness" that they saw in Jazzy's family that, they didn't want to fight. They all wanted to give Jazzy and Miriam hugs, and wanted Nadine to leave. But, L.B. was feeling torn between, Nadine and Jazzy. Who was due his loyalty? Nadine was his party and smoking buddy. Jazzy was the one that gave him the courage and freedom of spirit to BE! She took him in when the majority of the neighborhood had casted him and JoJo out. It wasn't that hard to decide. He knew how unstable Nadine was when she got her head bad. She had even blasted him out and embarrassed him to get a laugh from her other hang out buddies on different occasions. He didn't like how she had just done Jazzy anyway. It was really lowdown to him for her to refer to her children as Bastards. Jazzy had taken in so many of the kids and adults alike that fell on hard times, or just needed a place to know that they were cared about or valued.

Just as Nadine was about to come back swinging on Miriam, L.B. grabbed her and told her that she had "started enough shit for one day!" She tussled and kicked, and cussed him out and all of the innocent by standers got cussed out too! She bellowed out about L.B. being wrong for holding her and letting a "child" knock her around. She ranted on about how much she hated him and how she wasn't going to ever forget this day!

Chapter 18

You Still Don't know?

Peter made the call to Big Mama's sister's house later in the day after all of the commotion had gone on. He asked her if she could cut her visit short to come be with us. She told him that she had heard of all of the mess that took place and was on her way anyway. “That damn Nadine been messy all of her black ass life! I don't know why Jazzy even fool with her the way she cuts up and always starting up shit everywhere she go! She just ain't never been no earthly good. Then, she got nerve to always be talking 'bout, 'she know that the Lord got huh a mansion in the sky'. Hell, gawd ain't gone let the likes of Nadine into his heaven!” Peter couldn't do nothing but laugh. He wanted Big Mama there with us because, mama was having some pains and feeling real tired. She figured it was because of the events of the day. But, Peter told her that she wasn't going to hold that baby too long with all of the crazy stuff that keeps jumping off around here. He had to go back to work for the night shift all week. He said that it would be just Jazzy’s luck to go into labor while he was on the night shift. She just let him fuss. She tried to get L.B. to hang around and finish his story to the cops to her. Peter told L.B. “If you don't take that jive on outta here!” Jazzy gave Peter a gesture that he understood to say, “Go easy on him. He is still grieving the loss of his dearest friend!” Peter looked at her, wanting to say some choice words to her. But, he changed his mind. Apparently, L. B. had changed his mind too. He said that he had cried enough about JoJo and to tell the dirty police about another dirty police wouldn't help get Ole Dude out no way! Peter left Jazzy in the hands of L.B.

The "Gang fight" fizzled out after everybody had had their fill of Nadine setting off her share of confusion. Jazzy told her that she knew her way home and she didn't care if she didn't show her face over there again for a very long time! Nadine snatched her hot can of what was left of her beer, and twist her tail off to her car mumbling something. You had to wonder if she was feeling more out done because, Miriam had decked her, or if she was feeling forsaken by the whole neighborhood, or, because she never got the chance to tell her version of what happened with those low down cops!

You know, there was something that didn't set right with me (as Big Mama would say). It was odd how Janice never told anyone about Officer Ross or Officer Gipson being at her house and her screaming about them raping her! Except Vivian perhaps? Vivian was totally the opposite of Janice, for them to be friends. Vivian was so timid and such a quiet girl compared to most of the girls in the hood. Janice was a loud mouth Hoochie that went for bad! You would think that she was just a bag of hot air. But, she was as savage as her bark! I had to wonder why Candy Man didn't mess with her. She was always showing off her little shape by wearing her clothes as tight as possible, and it was no surprise. Big mama said "the fruit doesn't fall far from the tree" anyway. Her mama sashayed through the projects just when all of the boys were out in the evening, and the few men that had stayed by their woman's side, were shaking their heads in disgust and shame. Some of the guys bragged on how she really had a more banging body than her teenage daughter! The older men of wisdom would try to show the younger ones that, she couldn't keep a man long enough "to help raise them kids", because, she was so busy trying to find another one to lay up with! Ain't nothing "banging" about that! But, I guess Ole Dude figured; their mama was grown. If she wanted to allow Candy Man to use her up and keep her high, "for free", then, what could he do? As long as he (Candy Man) didn't mess with his baby sister then, he would let him be. For now that is.

Back to Janice. She wasn't there in the crowd when Vivian was about to tell on the crooks. I mean the police. I know if Jazzy could be in the mix of the gang fight, she could have come out to see the mess she started among the whole neighborhood! She was trying to stay in the cut to keep from answering to everybody who the baby daddy is. Vivian is going to have to watch her back...and front now! She didn't quite spill it all out. But, the crowd heard enough to know that those cops had a part in what happened to Ole Dude, Janice, and JoJo! Janice almost drags Vivian around to be her ego stroker. They are as different as night and day though. Janice just uses her to make her look good. Vivian is smart, with a unique, exotic beauty about her. She doesn't have to use the makeup and junk that the other girls cake up on their face every day. She just had a natural, effortless beauty. Why she never spoke up for herself, and just allowed Janice to use her the way she did, is a mystery to everybody. People always say of her that, her being quiet is the reason we should be watchful of her. Because, it's the quiet ones like Vivian that are always creeping about doing stuff. She is the one most likely to steal your man. She's the one that is most likely to throw the rock and hide her hand. But, for some reason, Janice had her under her thumb. She could get her to do most anything for her! Even to keep her secret of the crooked cop's antics. But, with her fearing that Janice may lose her baby, she was overcome with so much emotion over the pain this cop had caused Janice that she could not hold it inside much longer. But, just how much did she know, or could she tell and be left untouched by all of the stuff that she really knew that went on up in that house?!

Between L.B. and Nadine's rant with the cops, plus Vivian's story, and what I saw... I was sure that was enough to help get Ole Dude out of jail. I was feeling hopeful again! But, something on the inside of my stomach still didn't feel right. I couldn't breathe for a few seconds and it was just long enough to scare me like it did when I would have nightmares. I would just lock up throughout my whole body! That's why I wet the bed so much. I had a nightmare almost every night as a child. The only difference in this time is, I was wide awake and gripped with such fear for what was a mystery to me. I would soon find out though. I tried explaining it all to Big Mama. But, she just gave me her typical

"God answer". She said that monsters weren't real anyway. That was just the devil trying to bully me. So, my question was, "Why would God make a devil that went around bullying little kids and causing them to wet the bed and get whippings when they did?" she said that that was one of those other things that God would show me "By and by". I was so tired of hearing that excuse when I needed my type of questions answered! I marched straight out of the front door to my tree.

I hadn't been out there a whole lot since Dummy wasn't able to be there. I really believe it's because, I felt like God wasn't speaking to me anyway. I sho didn't feel like He was doing anything to stop all of the heartache in my world. He seemed to have taken the Tylers away from my life; Jeremy probably wasn't going to ever change anyway. So, I don't care that he was taken away. Dave still wasn't coming around. And, as much as I hated her sometimes, I still wanted Nadine to come around. She did try to comfort me after the military guy wounded my heart so much. She was really willing to come and help us fight the bullies. I just saw everybody leaving our lives. Peter came and everybody started leaving it seemed. I know he was not the reason for it. But, I was certainly thinking that people would see the goodness that Peter bought to our lives and want to be around him. I at least thought the Tylers would be doing things with mama and Peter nem. Well, I needed some answers still.

Now, this thing with Vivian, Janice, Ole Dude, JoJo, his brother, and these crooked cops was gonna get handled. Because, enough had gone on in this neighborhood at the hands of these low down policemen! The preachers were shaking hands and turning aside to the mess that they slithered around like snakes doing. As if they didn't see or have any idea of the dope deals the rape of the young girls...and boys at their hands! The preachers got called upon to counsel and pray with the children that were going through mental break down and shut down because of the way they were being violated in the shadows by these dogs! They knew that this poison was going on! They just accepted the "donations" that they put in the offering down at the church, when they came in only to place the offering in the bucket and using their presence to intimidate the victims of their evils every now and again. They knew the parents that saw them and wasn't afraid of them! Jazzy being one of them! The problem was having solid proof of what they were doing. The children felt it did no good. Teachers didn't want to stir the waters. They just wanted to keep their hands and good name clean. I was getting sick in my stomach thinking about the stories that I had overheard the grown folk talking and whispering about what these cops had done. I heard Big Mama say one time, "God got a day that he gets tied of his chilren being mistreated." I was wondering when He was going to get tied?

Chapter 19

Well, He Got Tied

You know that night at the Social when Janice was seen over in the corner, back in the dark with JoJo's brother? Well, "Old Dude" knew his sister was fast. He knew that she was always putting herself out to some boy! So, it was no surprise that Janice was cornered off smooching with JoJo's brother while her dance group was supposed to be in back stage practicing before they were supposed to perform. When the lights went out, something went awful wrong. The cops were slithering throughout the social here and there. So, no one paid much attention to them. The thing Vivian tried to get out of her mouth was, Janice had been making passes with her body at Officer Ross whenever she was flouncing around the neighborhood...just like her loose mama would do for these men around the neighborhood. But, she didn't expect it to go this far! She didn't know that Officer Ross was the one that was going to be behind the big water fountain at the back of the school. The one that Officer Gipson had plotted to have her meet up with him. She had already been instructed to ease out of the house after dark as it was. She was thinking that he had something grand to "reward" her with for snitching on the "Pusher man" in the neighborhood. She thought that she was going to be "rewarded". As she crept throughout the hood, and over the bridge...in the dark to see if Vivian could come with her; she didn't realize that she was being followed. Vivian's mom greeted her at the door of her house. "Where do you think you're going young lady? No, where do you think that Vivian is going this time of night? Does your mom know where you are?" She had so many questions that Janice just hurried away from her door with her yelling behind her, "You better get yo fast tail back over that bridge!" She just kept going toward the school. She got there and saw no one. That was spooky. She was expecting to see Officer Gipson with her..."reward". "Hello?" she said. She heard a voice from behind the big cement block. "Are you alone?" That didn't sound like Officer Gipson! She got nervous. "Gipson" Gipson was nowhere around. Ross stepped out from behind the block. . "Wha...who's there?" "Hey

Sweetie." Ross said in his overgrown tail voice. "What's going on?" Janice whimpered in fear. She knew that this was not the plan. She felt somewhat safe with Gipson. But, she ALWAYS got a Leary feeling about this one. Why was he calling her "Sweetie" in that tone? He saw and heard her fear. "Don't be nervous, you know I won't do you no harm. I came to "reward" you remember?" I know you were expecting Gipson. He uhh, he had something to come up." I am gonna be giving you your "reward". Janice knew from the sound of his emphasis on "reward', that there was something wicked in the plan. She rose up with indignation all in her chest! "I don't know what kind of game you and Gipson call y'all self playing. But, I ain't got all night to be out here befo my mama starting wondering where um at! So, whatever "Reward" you got fa me, you need to gone give me mine. I ain't come for nothing else but that!" Ross pulled her in closer to him and had a grip on her arm that let her know that he had other things in mind. She tried to pull back and resist him. "Oh, um gonna give you just "what you came fa." He made mockery of how she spoke. She didn't find it funny at all. She took her knee and did just what her mama had taught her. She put all of her might into it and, let him have it right in the "spot" as we were taught to call it when Jazzy taught us how to make a boy or man get up off of you long enough for you to RUN! That's exactly what Janice did. Ross doubled over in agony and called Janice every name under the sun, except what her mama had named her! She was running so fast and hard, she ran into Ole Dude like a bolder had hit him! It didn't even faze him. He was solid, big and dark as the night. She didn't even know that he was following her. She dropped to the ground in terror! Only because, she didn't know who she had slammed into! Her mind was whirling! She just knew that Ross could not be there in front of her that quickly! She left him mortified and in agony just seconds ago! Ole Dude grabbed her up like a rag doll and shook her! "What happened to you?" She was trembling and out of breath. She couldn't speak at first. He was still shaking her and asking the same question. She finally collected herself enough to get out "Ross". She pointed in the direction she had just escaped from. He dropped her. He stalked back to where Ross was, didn't ask one question. But, just proceeded to beat him to a pulp! He didn't play about his baby sister!

Janice had run as fast as she could to come back and see what had happened. Ole Dude was storming his way in her direction huffing and puffing with fire in his eyes. She didn't know if it was her turn or what. She stopped in her tracks to face him. He never lost a stride in his steps. He grabbed her by her arm and snatched her around, and was practically dragging her in the direction of home! When they had gotten to the bottom of the bridge her big brother stopped, stood her up straight in front of him, and looked her square on in her eyes. "None of this happened tonight. Do you understand me? Nothin happened tonight. No matter what he tells you he is going to do to you, me or mama...didn't none of this happen tonight. You hear me Guh?! "But, he's the Police....and, and, he could lock you and me up!" "You should've been thinking about all of that when you brought yo ass out the house, trying to be slick!" "I was coming to get my "Reward" from Gipson!" He told me to meet him behind the water fountain, after it got dark good." Ole Dude slapped her so hard her mouth started bleeding and she started swirling and swooning in the head! He grabbed her arm, ripped her dress on the back and bottom of it, pulled her hair all over her head, pushed her down in the grass and dirtied her hair up, her knee was scarred, and she thought he was losing his mind! Until, he explained their plan. He had her lurk behind long enough for him to get home and closed up in his room as if watching TV all evening. Then, she would limp in like she was all hurt and somebody had grabbed her up when she was trying to go to Vivian's to get her book for school, and they followed her, and tried to rape her, but she couldn't tell who it was because, it was dark and it was two guys. The one was trying to hold her and the other was trying to get her dress off. She tussled with them and was able to get her knee to one of them, and run, and she heard the man that let her get away being cussed out and getting punched around by the other as she ran into the distance to get away from them. That was going to be her story.

Ole Dude had to tell Janice that their story would work because, Ross was off duty, out of uniform, in the dark, in a place where no one else was there to see, or say so, Janice couldn't make out who he was if he did try to bring it up later. All she had to do was keep denying having seen him. He was not gonna want to admit to being whipped by a young girl or her big brother. Nor, was he going to want to admit that he came there with intentions to "Reward" her for Officer Gipson. That would put Gipson on the spot to answer for it, at least not for right now anyway. Because, it was still in Janice's mind, and her big brother's mind that Gipson was gonna pay for setting her up like this in the first place.

Now, if Janice could just remember to get the story about the school book just right with Vivian, and continue to deny that she even had a clue about what Ross would say about her and Ole Dude. Now, if it was me...I would be too embarrassed to say one word about it. Ross on the other hand, was a very cocky and arrogant type. He also was Gipson's flunky.

Now, the convincing Vivian was no problem at all. Vivian's mom had already yelled all that evening about how "someone was gonna rape or kill...or both that child, or her mama, if they didn't stop running these streets!" By the time Janice had made her story to Vivian, Vivian's mindset was different. She was thinking that they should've told it on Ross and Gipson. She felt that it would help to explain Ole Dude beating up a crooked cop. Gipson could get his too, for masterminding the whole meeting for Ross to go there with the intention of trying to have Janice against her will in the first place! What Vivian failed to realize was, no crooked cops were going to arrest other crooked cops! This just shut Vivian down in spirit. She felt like what's the use in trying to have any kind of dignity about you if it was not going to be honored or protected anyway. Her mom had forbid her to continue running with Janice anyway; Many times. She told her how it was making her look bad to be running with the likes of her. "People are going to be looking at you the same way they look at her...as a 'Tramp'.". Vivian's mom did not know the other side of Janice. She had a big heart for her family when they were around the house with each other. Janice had said that, "When you are outside of the house, you can't let people out there think that you're too soft." Her mom didn't know how Janice had taken up for her so many times when the boys had taken Vivian's quiet, gentle ways to mean that she was Easy and that they could just have their way with her. Janice had to call in her big brother a couple of times for Vivian. They embraced her as their "Little Sister". Her mom was not even going to hear of that! She didn't even allow her to be at Janice's house when she came home from school. If Vivian didn't see Janice out in the block, when everyone was hanging out, she was forbidden to be at her house! Her mom knew that Janice's mom was out street walking or laid up...according to the word in the neighborhood. So, why would she want her daughter in the midst of that type of upbringing? She told Vivian, "If you lay down with dogs, you're gone rise up with fleas". Vivian felt like all of that wasn't necessary to keep telling her. She knew that she didn't want to get pregnant and she wanted to go to college. So she knew to keep herself from the guys that Janice had tried to push off on her. They all thought she was "stuck up", and they had passed that reputation around the hood that she was not going to "put out" nothing! That was her determination, and she stuck by it without turning back! She was not going to mess up her future for Janice and nobody else!

Janice wanted to go to Gipson and jump his old low down tail for the trick he played on her! She was so confused though. If she went to him that would be admitting that she was there that night with Ross. She would be made to admit that her brother was there, and had put a sho nuff whooping on Ross' ugly butt! She wanted her "Reward"! Even after he had shown her that he was up to no good in the first place! Her mindset was like so many of the women and young girls in the hood. They never had any more to look forward to in their minds, except the hand out that this life "promised" to them. They thought that their body was their insurance policy to get what they wanted from men. So, many of them followed in the footsteps of what they had seen their mamas do with the low life men that came through the hood to "score", whether to get the loose women, or to bring in the dope that got the women and young guys strung out on the drugs that, the Candy Man pushed on them! They used their pills and powder to get the women into bed, and used the same dope to make pushers out of their sons!

For some reason, Janice didn't like the drug scene. She always boasted about being on a natural high. I thought she was just crazy! The guys that dropped in our hood knew that they were wasting their time coming by "Ole Dude's" way. He had put the fear of God in them about his family! He never did a whole lot of talking. He was truly a man of few words. You could just look at him and you knew that you needed not to cross him. It showed in his eyes to just be about doing righteous deeds when you came by his house. Everyone wondered what he was so angry on the inside about. Somehow, I didn't. I could understand how he could be feeling on the inside. His dad left them, after years of beating him and his mother. he had a mama with a reputation in the hood that was not so clean and a sister that was fast following in the footsteps of her mama, to be just as loose, if not more loose! He was left to hold down the cares of the house by doing odd jobs for people that were sometimes afraid of him because of his strong, intense features. He had to fight only a couple of times for folk in the hood to get them straight on talking about his mama! He beat some guys up so bad for about talking about his mama, they didn't think they were gonna make it! They really had to take them to the hospital! They tried to put him in Juvi but, because the dudes were older than him, and it was two of them that was bullying him around, and talking about his mama...they just kept him overnight to cool off. But, that "Overnight, to cool off" counted against him as having to go to Juvi anyway! It was one thing to tell him that they "understood" him taking up for his mama's dignity, (such as it was). But, to still give him a record after saying that all they wanted him to do was come in and "Cool off", was just low down! And, all of this time had passed, and he just found out when he went to "Real Jail"! For something I just don't believe he did at all!

Now, Vivian was starting to feel a bit out of sorts with Janice. She didn't like lying to her mother, unlike Janice who found it easy to lie to hers. She knew that she had to somehow protect Janice from the stuff that Janice had confided in her about Officer Ross, and the dirty trick that he and officer Gipson had tried to pull on her. But, when she had heard "in the wind" about the "Pusher man" finding out that it was Janice who had "snitched him out", and that he was going to see to her family being wiped off of the map! This gave Vivian more fear than the crooked cops did! When you were born and raised in the hood, you quickly learned who the worst enemy was, to the least of your worries that one might be. Candy Man was one of the worst! He had everything and everybody on radar for his bidding. Except those that were raised in whole family households. For those where there was a consistent male figure in the households, he didn't bother them. Patsy had told us to stay clear of him. She said, "He goes for bad. But, he knows who to mess with. And, it sho ain't none of Jazzy's kids! He's a coward anyway! He knows that Jazzy keeps her piece on her! She will use it too!" she had to show an old "friend" of hers that you don't put your hands on Jazzy Jones! The law was quite nice to people where "self-defense was concerned. That's exactly what I was hoping they would see about Ole Dude.

Vivian was going to have to make some tough decisions about Janice and keeping company with her. She had two strong issues to think about. Janice was going to have to be watching over her shoulders for Candy Man to strike, or the crooked Policemen to strike. So many times there had been "discoveries" of young women found strangled and raped, young men found, bound and gagged with their "down there" parts in their mouths, covered with "duck tape"..(I know it's Duct tape!) But, that's what we called it in the hood! Anyway, with all of the terrible killings and rapes going on around this town.... Janice had better be thinking with her head instead of thinking that her body was the way to get what she wanted! Candy Man was brutal to women! He ate women like Vivian for lunch! Janice was no match for him either. Because, he didn't care anything about how pretty a girl was. He had watched one of the biggest drug lords of the dirty south burn his mom's beautiful, long, black hair off, and scorched her beautiful face with a blow torch! She had messed over his money, and played him with another lord from the next city over. Thinking that she would not be found out, she didn't try to get up out of the hood with the money. She just kept flashing her new this and that. Candy Man would never be able to forget the screams and pleas from his mom! They forced him to watch as they tortured her. She was left blind in one eye and that side of her face looked like it had been melted like a candle when it dripped down and dried. She was pitiful! She didn't even want to live any more. The only thing that kept her going was her son. He had made a vow to "get them back" for what they had done to her! She begged him, in vain to leave it alone. He was only 12 at that time. But, vengeance stirred in his heart night and day for his mom's torturers! He had nightmares about the scene being relived in his mind each time he tried to drift off to sleep. His mom was taken away for a long time to get healed and for her to get therapy for the blindness. She cried every day for her only son. She told them that, "They were going to get him and turn him out!" They would just tell her that "the law would take care of all of that." Indeed it did. The law put drugs in his hands and tried to use him to help get the "bad guys" off the streets. Well, 32 years later...many drug addicts made later, many mysterious morbid deaths later discovered, many born addicted babies later, and Candy Man with a hatred for pretty women later. We can clearly see what The Law did for the little boy, given the nick name by the crooked cops of, "Candy Man".

Candy Man, Vivian? It was if she was being shielded somehow by a power beyond her heeding her mother's words of warning or advice. Because, she didn't take heed to her mother's word. So, it wasn't because, she was so obedient. But, there was still this nagging thing in my chest about why Ole Dude, his mom and his sister Janice had all had encounters with Candy Man. But, Vivian had slipped through his fingers. She was never around or just left the house when he came around to "collect" from Roxy. Ole Dude never liked it one bit when he came over! But, Roxy warned him to "Stay out of his way! I know what I have to do." So, she would close up in the room with him; and do what she ***had*** to do. Ole Dude just left the house in rage! Janice stayed in her room with the radio blasting so she wouldn't hear what was going on with her mama.....

Chapter 20

Warning Goes Before Destruction

No one noticed the fact that the cops had eased over to the back stage area of the school. The only ones that were supposed to have been back there was the ones participating in the Dance off because the girls were changing into their costumes and all. JoJo thought he was a girl too so, it didn't matter that the girls changed in front of him. The cops were supposed to be working the floors and the outside of the Social. JoJo's brother had been seduced away from Janice. He was told that his brother needed him backstage. They didn't think anything of it. They were smooching forever in that corner it seemed! So, it was a chance to take a breather anyway. So, somewhere in the middle of JoJo and Miriam's set being finished, and Raymond's and Malcolm's set rounding up their finish, Janice and her team setting up was supposed to be in motion already. But, something went wrong. Chaos broke out! Now, here's the thing. JoJo was not even the intended target.

Ross had a thing for Janice so badly! He wanted her, and didn't care what it took to get her. She looked upon him only as a money opportunity. She flaunted her body at him, made eyes at him, and got him that close! Then she would saunter off in mockery at him. It was not much he could do about it. Because, there was always the other girls in the hood around, or JoJo's brother trying to suck the life out of her mouth and pawing on her every chance he could get with her! Ross had had his fill of lurking around in his squad car to seek an opportunity to "get next to her" as they called it when someone wanted you to give up the goods and be their woman or man. Ross was determined to get Janice! He just didn't plan on JoJo being there behind stage and JoJo trying to block the first deadly blow to keep it from hurting his little brother!

Lights out! Ross makes his attack! Chaos back stage! Girls screaming, bodies colliding into one another, some falling, some getting trampled, and leotards, tutus and tap shoes flying all through the air!

Panic and pandemonium was the state of the Social Dance contest! There were little kids crying and trying to find their big sisters or brothers. Teachers and police were trying desperately to bring order to a bad situation!

Here's the problem. It was Janice and her crew's time to perform. When all of the trouble started, lights all out, Ole Dude was trying to get to the back stage area to find his little sister too! That placed him back stage when JoJo was taken down! He's big, and strong! He was not back there for any reason but, to get his sister Janice! Just like everybody else was trying to get theirs. So, why was he being accused of murdering JoJo?! He had nothing against JoJo! He had actually put the neighborhood bullies in their place about teasing him and L.B.! They were grateful friends to Ole Dude.

When you're dealing with crooked cops and under the table dealings of these guys; you don't even get to consider what motive a person has for doing anything. Because, they are going to build a case for you anyhow! Ross and Gipson were gonna get theirs though!

Malcolm and Raymond were yelling our names, and Miriam was coming up right behind me, Deginna, Sharletta, and Sasha. Mama and Nadine had given us the orders before we even left the house! "Y'all better stay yo skace tails together at ALL times! Don't go NOWHERE without the other! In fact, get your tails in one corner and stay there together! Tell Miriam where y'all are gonna be!" We were so afraid that we were hand in hand trying to get back stage to find Miriam, and she was trying to find us. By the time she got to us, and pulled the back of my shirt, the lights back stage came on. My eyes were strained at first. Then, I saw him...JoJo balled up on his side clutching his stomach, not moving, but, you could see blood up under him all over the floor! We screamed; fell to the floor with weakness. Miriam was trying to grab us and shield us from what we saw. It was too late. She tried to drag us away from him and I was pulling back to try to get closer to him. I needed to touch him to try to wake him up! I could hear Malcolm and Raymond yelling our names in the distance. Miriam yelled to them that we were, "Back here." They came running and out of breath. Then, they saw him too. Malcolm did a turnaround as if to run the other way. But, he saw Raymond double over and gasping for air! He started shaking him and beating on his back, and telling him to "Breathe Raymond, breathe!" He rose up and caught his breath and fell down on JoJo to try to turn him over. Miriam grabbed him and told him that it was already too late. We all just broke down all together in tears. Malcolm did too.

By the time the parents and the children had connected, they had handcuffed Ole Dude and carried him away. No questions asked of anyone! He was not that easy to take away though. He put up a good fight! We were all yelling, "What did he do?" Why are you doing him like that?" No one was trying to see about JoJo either! Jazzy was pitiful! Nadine was acting a plum fool! We just cried until we couldn't anymore, L.B. had to be carted off when the ambulance finally did come. He looked at his best friend lying there in a pool of blood, lifeless. He could not register it in his heart or mind. So, he just shut down. Patsy was ready to fight any and EVERYBODY! Miriam had to help collect everything and all of us kids and get us home, while Jazzy and Nadine waited for JoJo's brother to be found so someone could let him and his mama know that JoJo was gone....where was his baby brother and where was Janice now?

As we were walking home in silence, except for the sound of our cries, we could hear the other children talking about all of the events of the night and whispering about us being the family that had taken the "sissies" in. Raymond was too weak to even fight, or get back with them about calling our friends "Sissies". As strange as it may seem, my mind kept going back to Ole Dude. How could they possibly believe that he was the one that did this to JoJo?! What could they be doing to him now? I didn't know how to sort all of this out. Where was Janice, and why didn't anyone see Vivian anywhere all night? Officer Gipson was overly attentive. He used to let Ross be out front doing all of the work. Ross was mysteriously gone from the area that we saw him go back stage to before all of the chaos jumped off. When Jazzy and Nadine finally made it back home, I could hardly wait to tell her all of these things that I noticed that were going on at the Social. I didn't get to though. Police were flying throughout the streets of the hood, sirens whirling and flashing in the dark of the night, people running to and fro! This was not the time that I or Raymond could tell what went down.

L.B. had been held back for questions. What good that would do would be very little according to Jazzy. They didn't even try to let him get stabilized! I heard her fussing and cussing with Nadine agreeing with her that, L.B. was way too upset to be answering questions, when his best friend has been laid down!?

By the time that we all got in and settled, Miriam broke down! JoJo was just before them clapping, "Tap 2, 3, 4, break, twist, pop, heel, toe, step, and ball chain STOP!" "How could this be? He's gone!" That was all she kept rocking back and forth on the edge of her bed saying. Almost like a chant or mantra or something in her voice. I went to put my arm around her shoulder to try to comfort her, but Nadine came through just as my arm was midair to reach out to her. She snatched my arm and told me to, "Get yo frail tail somewhere and leave folk alone! If she wanted a hug she woulda told ya she did! You always trying to comfort somebody!" Miriam jumped up and pulled my arm away from Nadine, pulled me under her arm and told her, "Don't do her like that!" Nadine was about to say some more smart mouthed junk when Jazzy walked into the room. She told her, "Nadine, I thought I made myself clear about this one right here! You are not going to continue to try to break her spirit and make her stop having a heart for hurting people because your mean ass is so miserable! Now; I meant what I said! Stop messing with Monia before I have deal with you for real!" By then, Miriam had straightened up and was looking Nadine square in the eyes too! Nadine just did what she had always done. She walled her eyes at Jazzy and sashayed on out of the room mumbling, "I ain't no mo miserable than nobody else 'round here!" "You heard what I said." Miriam was in poised to fight mode. Jazzy just patted her on shoulder and told her that she was okay. "Come on Monia." she gave me a gentle nudge towards her bedroom. I knew that it meant that she wanted to talk to me about something serious.

"What happened at that dance Monia?" I always wanted to be totally understood so, I started at the front door to the back stage events. Jazzy usually tells me to go ahead and get to the point already. But, this time, she told me to take my time and try to remember as much as I possibly could about the events of that night. I told her of the police all lurking around, how Ross and Gipson eased to the back stage while them girls were back there getting dressed, and undressed. I told her of how we had seen Teddy get called to the back by Gipson when Janice and him were in the corner smooching all night. Then, he got called to the back when Janice had to go get changed to her dance outfit. I told her that I know she said not to move from the spot that Miriam put us when we got there. But, I could tell something wasn't right behind that stage, and I needed to know what it was. So, I was the one that made Sasha and nem come back there with me. Then, the lights went out, and we heard a yell of bad pain from somebody! Then, there was a thump of something or somebody hitting the floor. Someone running and knocking people and stuff over, a bunch of screaming and then the lights came on, and we were standing right by JoJo's body on the floor in a whole lot of blood! Ross was gone, Gipson was gone, and so was Teddy! Before they came to get JoJo, the other cops were wrestling Ole Dude down to the ground to put hand cuffs on him. Janice and everybody else was screaming, and wondering why they were taking him away in hand cuffs, "He didn't do nothing! Why are y'all doing him like this?" We didn't know whether to cry for JoJo or Ole Dude! Jazzy said, "So, you mean to tell me that Ross and Gipson were gone when the lights came on?!" I gave a big nod up and down of my head. She lit a cigarette, folded her arms across her chest and told me to go on in the room and be with the other kids for now. You could tell she had some serious stuff on her mind!

When I got in the room, Sasha was sitting there with her old soggy thumb in her mouth, looking at me like, "Well?" I didn't open my mouth! "What Jazzy say?" I told her if she wanted to know she would just have to go ask her herself! She jumped down off of the bed and proceeded to do just that. Before she could get in the door of Jazzy's room, Jazzy told her, "You just march yo little tail right on back in there and leave me alone! I need to think about this thang a minute!" Sasha ran back to the room so quick! Because, she was so shocked when Jazzy snapped on her lil tail! We laughed so hard that we forgot about being sad about JoJo for a minute! She ran around the room and made her rounds of pinching each one of us that she could get to for laughing at her! Boy! We had a blast with that one! Sasha was boiling! I was so glad to see her get hers for a change!

I don't know what it is about Jazzy's house. But, every time there's something jumping off in the hood, the officials want Jazzy's perspective about it. We were wayyy late into the night getting to bed! Ross and Gipson didn't come to the house to ask more questions. But, some officer that we hadn't seen up through these parts of the hood before now came to our house. I don't know why somebody up at that station didn't warn him about Jazzy. He came in all fast talking and trying to march up into our house like he lived there and got stopped cold, in his tracks by Jazzy. "Uhhh, I know that you don't think you coming up in MY house without a warrant in your hand!" "Ma'am, I just need to ask you a few questions." As Jazzy stood boldly in front of the officer to block him from coming into her door, she put her hand out to stop him. "You can ask all of the question you think you want to ask right over there on the other side of that door. Ain't nothing up in here you need to be checking out while you asking your questions." We all stood right behind her and eyed him very closely. I was as brave as I wanted to be when I was with my mama. Because, she wasn't scared of nothing but worms and creepy crawlers! She was afraid of nobody! But, there was that one officer that I was terrified of! All mama had to say was, "Here he comes!" She didn't even have to get his name out of her mouth. I was running in terror into the house! I don't know what it was about this officer. Because, I hadn't ever really seen him directly just passing in the patrol car at a distance!

"I know my damned rights ya hear! You ain't setting a foot up in here unless you got some papers in your hand! Now, what you want here at my house? Every time something jumps off around here, y'all are running over here like I'm the town crier or something! You need to be up at that school trying to find out how the staff up there let things get so out of hand and now my friend is dead!"

You didn't see Jazzy cry about much. But, she couldn't hold back the tears at this point. "Well look ma'am; I can see that you're in no shape right now to talk to me. I will just check back tomorrow some time if that's okay with you?" Jazzy just nodded her head and closed the door as he walked away. We all wrapped around her with hugs and tears as well. That was a long sad night.

Morning came with a blare of phone calls, and people knocking at the door to come see if we were all okay. They knew how we all were about JoJo. Malcolm was as mean as a bear that morning. He didn't want ***nobody*** to say nothing to him, or get in his way! Mama told us to just leave him be. She knew he was feeling bad because he couldn't do anything to help JoJo. Raymond was feeling just as bad. Miriam wouldn't even get out of the bed. When she did, she went to the bathroom and was dry heaving. She had cried herself to sleep and threw up until she couldn't any more. Mama told her she was going to mess around and get too dehydrated! She kept making us take her water and popsicles.

Everyone that Jazzy felt was cool was at our house that morning. Big Mama was trying to keep coffee going for the coffee drinkers, and guess who showed up that day? Dave! That's right. Dave! The only difference was, where he used to come over before with his beer in his hand, half drunk; this morning he came over with a bible in his hand and very sober! He was so pleasant and peaceful! The last time I remembered seeing him there was when Nadine had made him feel so bad, he was crying and feeling forsaken by ALL of his friends! I remembered telling him that, "It didn't matter if he didn't have any friends because, Jesus would be his friend when no one else would." Remember? Well, there stood a new man that was a friend of Jesus! I was oh so happy to see him again! It made the morning seem brighter. He said that he came because, he'd heard what happened to JoJo and he wanted to offer prayer for those that wanted it.

Well, things went a little bit different this time. Nadine had swallowed her pride from the night before and made it over early Saturday morning as it was her custom to do if she wasn't out on the fish creek. The last time, she had cussed Dave out and told him that folk wasn't up to him always coming around drunk and crying early in the morning. Remember? Well, time and struggle has a way of changing "folk". Nadine was the first person to jump up and want prayer from Dave! Everybody's eyes almost popped out of their heads! Nadine wanted prayer?! Dave didn't act at all surprised. He got his bible and asked her could he show her something before they prayed. She said, "Nah Dave, Nah. Wait one minute. I need to ask you to forgive me first before you open up the "Good Book". I ain't 'bout to be touching or gazing on the Lord's word after the way I treated you the last time I laid eyes on you! I ain't gone do it I tell ya!" Dave told her, "Now, for what it's worth, I forgave you that very day Nadine." "You did?" Yes I did Nadine. See, the Lord showed me in his Holy word that very day; if I wanted to be forgiven of my sins, I had to forgive others. I was looking for the way they said Jesus taught the disciples to pray. When I read it, the Lord told me to keep reading. So, I did. And that's what I stumbled up on. See Nadine, not only was I mad at you, I was hurting inside from a whole lot of other stuff. Some of it, I brought on myself. Some stuff was done to me by so many people over the years. When I cried out to God about the mess my life was in, the Lord pointed me to Jesus, and I started reading in Matthew, I just picked up my old bible and dusted it off, and I started reading like a mad man! The more I read, the more I wanted to read! Then, I prayed that prayer in the 6 chapter of Matthew. As soon as I said, "Amen", I heard, "Keep on reading." The very next two verses told me where I was in my heart Nadine!" "What you mean Dave?" He said, "Let me show you." Not only did she draw closer to him at the table with his bible, most everybody in the room gather around to see what he was talking about. He turned to the 6th chapter of Matthew and pointed out the 14th and 15th verses. When he read it out loud to all those listening in; they all looked from one to the other and back at Dave. Nadine just hung her head in shame, and tears were rolling down her face. Some of the others were very sad looking too. Dave just put his arm around Nadine shoulder and told her that it's okay, and he and the Lord forgives her. Others in the room stepped up and said they wanted prayer and to forgive this person or the other. They even made up with some in the room that didn't even know that one was mad at them! It was so warm and loving in Jazzy's house that morning. Big Mama said, "Lord, it took Dave sobering up, to brang chuch to Jazzy's house! 'Cause Jazzy sho won't gone go to that chuch down the way over yonder!" Mama said, "Well, you know I am not about to let Nadine out shine me with the Lord! I guess I'm gonna have to forgive them folk down there at that church too!" Nadine, laughed, and came over and hugged Jazzy, and then, reached down and pulled me close to her and said, "You are some kind of special lil girl! Can you find it in your heart to forgive Aunt Nadine?" I just nodded and gave her a waist hug. Dave begins to praise the Lord and the others in the room did too. Dave begins to give his story about how his life had been since he was last there. He had all of our attentions at that point. Jazzy got a cup of coffee and a cigarette. Dave said, "Jazzy, I am not trying to tell you what to do. But, your body is the temple of the Holy Ghost and the Lord don't want you to be smoking them cigarettes. I ain't trying to tell you how to live. But, the word done told us that, if we do stuff to destroy the temple, the Lord will allow the thing we use to do it, to destroy us. We have to have our body to house God! If you keep smoking, you are destroying your body, and possibly your baby's body too." She put the cigarette down slowly and looked him straight in the eyes. She said, "Dave, you know what? You are exactly right. I got to stop this mess! The Lord has been too good to me. I can't keep abusing HIS body!" That spoke to the silence in the room. Nadine looked a little troubled. She said, "Now, Dave, I get the forgiveness thang, and all that about our body being the temple and all. But, hell....I like smoking my joints and dranking my beer!" Everybody busted out in laughter, and giving each other Dap! They knew that Nadine was going to bring up her Reefer! Everybody knows how she loves her beer! Dave just laughed, dropped his head and shook it in silence for a few minutes. Then, he spoke. "Nadine, you're partly right." She looked surprised. She thought he was giving her a pass on smoking her Weed, over Jazzy smoking her cigarettes! Not so! What Dave was saying was, Nadine was doing right in being honest with her heart before God. She knew that she wasn't ready to stop doing these things. She knew that she needed God and His forgiveness. She also knew that there were things she could honestly say that she was not ready to give up. Like so many of the rest of them in the room. Dave was trying to show us that God saw us just where we were and STILL wanted us to be His children, and to come to Him! I couldn't understand why God could love us so much!? Dave told us the story of Job. Then, he told us the story from the New Testament about the Lunatic in the grave yard. This helped us to see how the devil does a person from the ones that are trying to do right, to the ones that can't even help themselves. That was where Nadine could relate to him better. She knew she wanted to be a better person. She knows that the beer and weed made her act out, or like she just didn't care about nobody but herself whenever she smoked or drank. She just didn't know how to stop! Well, her day of visitation was TODAY!

suit that came in with Ole Dude. He was trying to get

After Dave had explained how it took God in the Old Testament to speak a word that it was "ENOUGH"! Then, did we understand that, when God comes to see about you, the devil has to let you go! Sometimes you can be minding your own business and the devil will show up to try you, just like he did Job in the book of Job. You don't have to be bothering nobody. But, Big Mama said it like this. "Ole Slue foot gone stick his big head up errtime!" Now, this man in the grave yard, I still don't understand why he was like he was. But, I know when Jesus showed up, He made him alright! Dave said he was "Clothed in his right mind." I asked him, what it meant to be "Clothed in your right mind"? He said, "The devil finds a way to get into your thinking process, and have you so kooky in the head that he brings as many bad thoughts and ways for you to get caught up in mess that ain't no weed, no beer, no drugs or nothing can fix yo mind! It takes Jesus to get on the case, and show you just how bad off you have become! That's what had to happen to the Lunatic. That's what they called the Man." But, Dave showed us something about that. He showed us how Jesus said *he had to* go to the other side of the water to another town, instead of where his friends that followed him all of the time thought they would be going. But, Jesus knew what He was supposed to be doing long before he met these men that he called his friends. He had to go to the other side to see about the man that ran out of the grave yard to meet him as he was coming off of the boat. The people said he was doing so much crazy stuff to others and himself that; they had to lock him up in chains to keep him from hurting himself! He had lost his mind! But, when Jesus came, the little bit he had left knew that if he could just get to Jesus, he would make him alright! Dave said that the evil spirits that were in the man were trying to ask Jesus if he had come to bother them "before the time?" He said, Jesus told them to "shut up!" He said, that Jesus talked to the evil spirits and asked what their name was, and they answered him, and told him that their name was, "Legion" because there were so many of them that had gotten in the man's body and mind! Dave said that was like 3000 to 5000 thousand evil spirits in one man's body! I couldn't even begin to imagine that in my little brain at the time! All I know is, I was so happy when Dave said that, by the time Jesus got through with them, they had to leave and go off into some pigs that were standing close by! I didn't care about no pigs! But, guess what? Them crazy people got mad at Jesus! They were so worried about how they couldn't make no money selling them pigs, instead of being glad that the man was back to his right mind and free from the devil and his imps trying to destroy this man's life! Dave said, "I am not lying! It's all right here in the 5th chapter of Mark!" They all leaned forward to see what he was showing them.

Long story short; Dave was showing the different ways the devil can come to your life, and it takes you seeing and admitting where you really are in your life and letting the Lord help get you straightened out! Because; Job was a righteous man in God's eyes. But, he still needed the Lord. Dave could never explain why the man in the grave yard was like he was, or why so many evil spirits were in him. Except that he said a "door" was opened in his life somewhere by him or his parents at some point in his life or theirs by what they were living day to day. That's all he had to say for Nadine! She didn't want no Boils on her, and she didn't want to have no devils all up in her body and mind! She wanted to know what she had to do to be Free! That's all Dave needed to hear!

When he shared all about the reason that Jesus came to set the captives free, she found it too easy to be true. But, when she heard the truth about what Jesus did to die for her sins, and rose from the grave to bring her into right standing with the Father, back to the beautiful place of fellowship that the devil had stolen from her. She and the rest of us were standing there with our mouths wide open! We didn't know that because of the love and mercy that God had for us that he would give his only begotten son so that we could be one of His children too! When, I heard that, I began to cry like a baby! They were not sad tears though. They were tears from being so overwhelmed with such amazing gratefulness, at how I could be so loved, and have the opportunity to have the Father of fathers for my daddy! God himself!

Chapter 21

JoJo's Justice

Dave "spoke over" JoJo's body at his funeral; along with a whole lot of folk that wanted to have "their say". Big Mama had to save hers for last. The first time she tried to speak but, had to be escorted to her seat because she became too overcome with sorrow to speak. I believe that, what Dave had to say helped her. He told us how there were those that had judged JoJo for be "Different". He said, "As far back as I can remember, JoJo had a heart of love for people and he tried in all he remembered to love the Lord as best as he could." Then, he had those with their Bible to turn to the book of Romans and read the 14th chapter aloud with him. By the time everyone finished, you saw some that dropped their heads in shame, some that looked puzzle about what this meant. Some were nodding matter of factly and amening to what they had read. Dave saw the question mark in our faces. So, he broke it down for us. He explained that, everybody's got a belief in their mind...(where ever they got it from) that one way is right and someone else's way of living for God or serving the principles of their faith in God is wrong. Simply because the person doesn't do things the way they do. He said, "Y'all just make sure that you let God be the judge of that person, and know that we all are going to stand before him to answer for ourselves for what we have lived or not lived." He said that, "He was not going to stand up there and preach JoJo into a Heaven or Hell that wasn't even his to ***let*** anybody into; one way or the other!" But, he did leave us with this. "Y'all better make sure that you be found loving like JoJo did. He didn't have no difference between one person over the other! He loved everybody the same. He would do whatever he could to help you. He would give you the shirt off of his back, and he did love the Lord. It showed in his life. He had a struggle with what y'all called "being different" But, he was trying! You could see it in his life! Now, um just crazy enough to believe that the Lord will show him his Great Mercy and his Great Grace! That's the same thing we ALL gone need on the day that we stand before Him. Before I take my seat, I want to leave you with this question. Will you be ready to meet Him when He calls your name?" Some people looked bewildered; some couldn't stand it any longer. Several people got up from their seats and asked what they needed to do to be ready.

There was a presence that day of JoJo's "Home Going" service that was almost too hard for me to describe. It was gripping, convicting and warm. JoJo would have been pleased that his service went in this way! You know, Jazzy and Big Mama were sad and happy at the same time! But, trying to stay neutral as Dave and the other Elders and Ministers began to have the people that stood up, to come forward, and give their lives to Jesus. Guess who came up from the back of the church to give their life to the Lord? Not Nadine. But, Vivian and Roxy! Can you believe it?! No one had seen Vivian in a while! Roxy had never been to a church before that day! But, they both came up almost on queue! A hush came over the service. Some of the people were standing there in disbelief, some with their mouths hanging open like, "how dare she!?" Dave took up his microphone and reminded the congregation that they had all just agreed that the 14th chapter of Romans was the best point to consider when we are tempted to judge people. That brought things back to order.

After each of the people had repented of their sins before everyone, and accepted Jesus as their new Lord, and Savior they asked each of the new converts if they would like to state their names, and if they had any brief words they wanted to share with the congregation. Well, Jazzy always said that, "when God comes into your life, He makes you want to 'DO' right." Well, I told you that Big Mama said that God has a day when He gets tired of his kids being treated wrong, and picked on. Something took a turn at JoJo's service.

I didn't forget to let y'all know what happened when Vivian, Nadine and me had something we needed to tell the crooked cops about what we saw the day when the "Bullies" were down in Jazzy's back yard and thought they were gonna whoop my mama's baby out of her! Well, I believe that it was all God that didn't let it come out then. Because, the crooked cops would have kept it from making it to the proper authorities and JoJo's murderer would not have been brought to justice. Well, Vivian had gone as far as she could holding her truth. Roxy was at a place that she was truly tired of herself and the life she had lived, all of the dark secrets she had kept for Candy Man, and all of the awful things she had seen done by him to people. Now, her son was serving a possible life sentence! She was just TIRED! Vivian had hidden behind a cloak of being the sheltered girl in the neighborhood. So, no one expected what she was about to say. But, before she could speak, there was a noise coming up from the back of the church. It was the sound of shackled feet, and several officers, and men in suits as well.

Ole Dude! I was happy as well as sad to see him. But, why was he here? Why would the murder suspect be at the victim's funeral?! "Something didn't jive" (as Patsy would say). When Vivian saw them coming down the aisle, she began to tell Dave and the others present that she wanted to tell her story that she didn't get to tell on that day. She testified about how good it felt to be in the Lord and free from the weight of living a lie! Everybody looked from one to the other in confusion. Janice was the first to ask, "What chu mean?" She went to open her mouth again, Roxy spoke out. "Lord knows that I have tried to do the best I could raising my two chilrin. I taught them right from wrong even if I wasn't living right. I didn't raise no "murderer!" Now, I have been hearing thangs out here on the streets about you being undercover Ms. Vivian. So, what you got to say for yoself?" Dave and the other Elders were about to try to set order in the church again. But, the Pastor of the church stepped in and said, "Let the young lady answer her." Dave stretched his arm out to point at JoJo, in an attempt to remind everybody that this was about JoJo. Vivian said, "This is about JoJo. I have kept this stuff as long as I can. I can't tell another lie ***to nobody***; I can't keep acting like it's you Janice that my reputation is being ruined by. I sure can't keep quiet another day while Ole Dude stays locked up and possibly get murdered in jail himself by those two sitting right over there in them "dress blues"; trying to look innocent and concerned for this community! I have been undercover indeed. Gipson and Ross your time is up in this town." Ross stood up and asked her, "Who the Hell you think you are?!" The pastor stood up and told Ross, "I know you ain't talking like that up in the house of the lawd!" Ross gave his attentions back to Vivian. "What chu talkin bout?" At that, Gipson stood up and added, while rolling his eyes between Vivian and the pastor. "Yeah Vivian, what the Hell you thank you talking about?" She kept getting a sign from one of the officers in the her to hold her story in. she blurted out to him, "I just made a vow to the Lord to live for HIM! I can't continue to lie and cover up this evil that's been going on for waayyyyy too long! Ms. Roxy, I know you are tired of covering up for these goons and Candy Man too!" She just broke down crying and dropped to her knees. Ole Dude couldn't stand to see his mama like that. He started trying to get to her to comfort her, and Gipson reached for his pistol, but Dave intercepted him and yelled, "He's just trying to comfort her! Stop in the name of Jesus!" Gipson just froze in his tracks! Everybody was captivated by the fact that Ole Dude was saved from being shot, by Dave commanding him to stop in the name of Jesus! The officers freed Ole Dude from their grip long enough for him to comfort his mama. She just held on to him for as long as they allowed her to. She kept repeating, "Lord save my child!" She was too weak to hold up any longer. She started telling of all the stuff that Candy Man had on Gipson and Ross. She told of how they had been threating JoJo's little brother, Teddy to say that he was the dad of the baby that Janice was carrying, when she knew all along that Gipson had raped her child, and tried to get her, and Janice to say that it was someone else's to keep Gipson from going to jail for raping a minor! When, JoJo overheard his brother, Teddy and Janice talking, he went and confronted Ross and Gipson about it. He recalled talking to L.B. about having seen Ross in plain clothes standing out around Janice's bedroom window when him and Nadine had been sitting out in the car getting high together, on my birthday to be exact! Because, I saw him too when I was trying to go get the new boy, Gill to see me in my new birthday clothes! I can see it before my eyes right now!

Candy Man had Roxy by the throat to keep quiet about it because, Gipson kept giving him "Stay outta jail" cards too because he had so much on him! Ross was a scaredy cat! But, Vivian had just taken it all in over the course of time. No one knew that there was a rat in the police department. We certainly didn't know that the "Big boys" were in on it! The Feds at JoJo's funeral! This was too much to handle! They had been using Vivian all along to help them! She said that she was "Through with the whole mess! If y'all can't get Ole Dude off from here, I will just have to tell Jesus on a whooole bunch of y'all crooks!" All of the time, we thought Vivian was timid and shy and soft spoken! She just took on the posture of dropping to her knees praying! She began to ask the Lord to forgive her for all of her part in this big mess! And, to protect all of those that are innocent in this town, so that they can come forth to tell of all the low down that "Candy man and Gipson, and his cohorts had done to them, and their sons and daughters. By the time she had finished praying and everybody had learned that the feds were among them to come and do away with Gipson and his crew; everybody started trying to tell their story one over the other! JoJo was long since forgotten about! But; Big Mama hadn't had her say yet! When she stood up, a hush came over the room. Everybody respected Big Mama!

"Now, Roxy, and Vivian and all of y'all up in here is wrong! Gawd ain't about no confusion in his chuch house, and all of y'all know it!" Jazzy folded her legs as best as she could with her belly being so big, nodded her head at what Big Mama said, and started fanning herself really fast! Dave took a stand over by the casket to show that he was on her side too. Big Mama continued to speak when she knew there was order. "Now, I'm gonna say my piece, and I'm gonna say what the lawd love. That's the TRUTH! Roxy, I ain't got no judgment for you! I could walk them street coners better than anybody ever walked up in these parts of town! Vivian, I got away with it because, I was sneaky just like you!" Vivian just dropped her head. "I did all I thought I was bad enough to do! Then, y'all round here wondering where Jazzy get her fiery ways from!" Everybody laughed! "Now, now, this young man laying here only fault was, he wanted folk to treat each other right! That's all he ever strove with us to do. He was fond of girly things, and hanging out with us at Jazzy's. Could pop that chewing gum so loud, and kept him some in his mouth. Yes he did. You could hear him coming, he popped it so loud!" Big laughter then! "But, he didn't deserve to leave this wurld like he did! It just breaks me down I tell ya! He brought so much joy and laughter into Jazzy's household! He thought he needed us to help him feel like somebody, when all the time, we needed him to come around and teach us how to be bold enough to own up to whatever it was we's about in this life! He taught us not to judge because, he never judge no one! He even loved those that were mean to him! So, we not about to sit here and make this all out to be about Gipson and them crooks over there! We came to celebrate JoJo, and that's what we gone do! Vivian, if you through praying, and having your say, get on up off of that flo, and get up there and sang JoJo's song!" Vivian wondered how she knew she sang, and especially how she knew JoJo's song! Roxy had been taken to her seat, the officers had allowed Ole Dude to pay his respects to JoJo, and the Feds had heard enough to back up what Candy Man had already told them because they had him in protective custody we would learn. He had stuff for old and new on Gipson and Ross! "Gwone on up there and sang that song gal!" Vivian sang, like an angel! She sang Mahalia Jackson's song, "Troubles of the world". There wasn't a dry eye in the place! Roxy was changed! She stood up and you could see the glow on her face! The heavy burden that was on her when she came to the altar to receive Jesus was washed away! She said something that made the same thing that Jazzy told me before make a lot of sense! She said, I have been doing some things that I am not so proud of. Some of you have too. Y'all know I ain't nevah been shame of nothing I do. But, I am not about to sit here and keep lying to God! I see everybody's face in here but, one. Everybody started looking around one to the other. You know who had eased in and eased on out? Candy Man. He was there, because I saw him for myself. Well, you know Jazzy said, "When Jesus comes into your heart, you just want to do right!" Roxy said, "I don't see him. But, God sure does. In fact, He saw all of the dirt he did, I did, and, you too Vivian!" A total hush came over the church.

Vivian rose to her feet with a look of terror in her eyes. She looked at Roxy with a begging look in her eyes. All eyes were on Vivian. The soft spoken, respectful, very pretty young lady, that had just sang the glory down, was in the spot light again. This time it was for all of the wrong reasons.

Candy Man had yo yoed Roxy for a very long time. He was several years younger than her. So, why was he able to dog her around so much? The times that he would show up at Roxy's house, were the times that Vivian was never around. There were many girls that had been "Handled" by Candy Man. Some very pretty, just like Vivian. He had done some very mean things to them. He cunned them to fall for him, being that he was a very handsome guy. Then, he hooked 'em! The girls in the Hood had children that were brother and sisters to each other all over the neighborhood! We lost count of how many kids he had with these women! He had some that he deliberately got strung out on the "Candy". Some that he would beat if he thought they were trying to mess with that life. He had his favorites that he kept a watch on by his "Boys". He had raped, tortured some of them by messing up their faces with cigarette burns, and made those with long pretty hair shave their own heads bald! There was even those he made to prostitute for him...Roxy was one of the few from that neighborhood alone. He was heartless!

Vivian's mom had made a point to always keep the reputation of being the "Upstanding Citizen in the hood". She made sure that everyone knew that she was cut from another cloth. One thing that itched was how; there was a striking resemblance of Vivian and Candy Man! Everybody's question was why is it that, of all the pretty girls that Candy Man had made his subjects, and victims, Vivian had been untouched by him. Guess why? You got it! She is his Sister! She was his cover, his babies' mamas' worst nightmare...that is, next to him! When they saw her coming, they didn't know what was about to happen to them! She pimped them out for her brother, slapped them around, razor slashed a couple of his girls across their face if they tried to threaten to tell on her or him! She would befriend them to get information out of one on the others. Then, watch as Candy Man dogged them out! All the while, it came out at JoJo's service that the "Upstanding" mama knew ALL of this stuff! So did Gipson, Ross, and Roxy!

The Feds had Ole Dude taken back to the car. The pastor and the funeral officiates were instructed to wrap up the service, and to get Jazzy and Big Mama out of the church. I was determined that I was able to stay with Miriam and Malcolm and be okay. I had to see the end of the matter. Jazzy just gave me that "look". I knew that I better not do ***nothing***! They proceeded to place handcuffs on Vivian, her mama, and Roxy. Gipson and Ross tried to step forward to assist them. The dudes with the big guns cocked them, pointed them straight up at Ross, Gipson, and the other cocky acting officer that had showed up a few times on calls, but stayed on guard for Gipson. The one that had been giving orders throughout the service gave the command to "Cuff 'em", said it with such authority and pleasure that the whole church jumped to their feet cheering, and putting up their Black Power fist and giving each other

Dap! Vivian's mama was fussing and cussing Vivian and Roxy out like a mad woman! All of her sadity ways went out the window! One of the girls that had a baby for Candy Man got ready to leave out of the church. But, she made it her business to walk close enough to Vivian and her mama, to spit on both of them before she walked out! The cops didn't even bulge to try to stop her! They had the whole story ran down to them from several of the mamas before they had even got there to pick up the crooks!

Teddy had been placed in protective custody as well. They were trying to make sure Gipson and Ross didn't get to him. Janice was so pitiful. She had to watch her mama being carted off, her brother, and the young man she loved was gone, and she had carried a baby that was fathered by a demon seed called, Gipson! What was to come of her life? Everyone was gone. She thought. As JoJo was laid to rest and everyone had gone on to the repasts, Janice had drugged her tired body on back to the house to the 4 walls of dread and gloom. She didn't even have the strength to see about how to try to bail her mama out. She was sure it was gonna be a good while before they got to a trial for Ole Dude. She imagined that Gipson was gonna deny and lie so much that they would take forever getting it before the courts to give him a fair hearing. I could not help but feel sorry for Ole Dude more than Janice. Because, Janice left her fast tail up for grabs to these different guys, until Teddy came along.

She cried most of the way home. As she went to open the door, the knob wouldn't turn, she was sure that she had left the door unlocked because she was coming back home and Roxy was going to stay for the repasts and go out later. You just didn't have to lock your door up when practically everybody in the hood was at the funeral. Even the Italian family, Miss Rosie nem was at the service for JoJo. She twisted the knob again. This time there was some help on the other side of the door. She jerked her hand back and turned to run. She was sure it was Gipson! She knew he had snaked his way out of everything else. So, why not this time too? Before she made a full turn, she was quickly pulled into the house to fall into the arms of her big brother, Ole Dude!

There had been enough reported, spied out, and verified information to have a grand jury indict the officers for the murder of JoJo and the rape of Janice and others at the hand of Gipson, Ross, Candy Man, and a couple of their other crooked partners too! They had to release Ole Dude!

Janice called Big Mama first. They both had a special place in their heart for her. Ole Dude wanted her to know that he was free! He said that she was the only one that came to see him other than Roxy, after Jazzy had gotten too big and feet too swollen to walk the halls of the prison to come see him.

When the call came, Big Mama was sitting there so sad and quiet. Jazzy had lain down sad and exhausted from all of the events of the day. It was so hot! We were lying on the floor on a pallet, with the fan blowing on us half asleep too. A scream went out so loud that, it made all of us jump straight up! Including Jazzy! Big Mama was crying tears of joy, dancing her "sanctified dance" and praising God! She never said a word for us to know what the call was about! Then, Jazzy was coming down the hall bent over and motioning for us to come to her. She was peeing on herself! Why didn't she go to the bathroom? Her room was right across the hall from the bathroom. But, something was different about her. She seemed very helpless. Miriam told me, "Go get Ms. Holly and Patsy!" Malcolm yelled to Bernard, "You go Bernard. You run faster!" That was all Bernard wanted to hear. He loved being the bearer of important news! Big Mama didn't know which way to go! She was trying to hear the good news from Ole Dude, and she was trying to tell them about Jazzy. She had to just drop the phone. She gave everybody's orders to them. She got Jazzy wrapped with a sheet around the waist, and between her legs. She sat her down, went back to the phone, only to find Ole Dude still talking. She said, "Boy, shut cho mouth and hang this phome up! Jazzy finna have this baby! I need to call Peter!" She didn't even wait for a reply from Ole Dude. We all laughed. I was left in charge of keeping stuff picked up from the floor while Mama was gone to have the new baby. Malcolm was in charge of keeping all of the trash taken out, and Bernard was determined to stay over our house to, "help out". So, he had to sweep and mop the floors, and Miriam had to keep the lunch packs fixed for us. Big Mama said that the hospital keeps you there for 3 days when you have a baby. I wondered what they had to do to have a baby!

Before Jazzy could even leave to go to the hospital there was a knock at the door. Ole Dude! I forgot all about my mama needing to get to the hospital to have the baby. She did too! She tried to get up to rush and hug him and caught a pain so hard it buckled her knees and she started dropping to the floor! Ole Dude lunged in and caught her just in time. He was big, and strong. Jazzy collapsed in his arms. Big Mama was pacing the floor back and forth when Patsy and Ms. Holly came in the back door. Patsy went into a frozen stop and stare when she saw Ole Dude. All he could say was, "Big Mama, what you want me to do with Jazzy? She getting heavy!"

Ms. Holly was the only one that had some calm about things going on in the room. She had been there for so many of the mamas in the hood with their babies. We were all still laughing with joy to see Ole Dude and hear him say anything! We all thought he was gone for good! I don't know if I was happier that Mama was finally having this baby or, that my silent friend was back home again! Ms. Holly yelled, "Boy, put Jazzy over there on the studio cot and get yo big black tail over here and give me a hug!" He did just that with the biggest smile on his face that all of us had ever seen on him before! He never smiled! We all ran over to him and hugged up on him too! He had a rush of deep breaths and tears to well up in him all of a sudden. Before long, all of us were crying tears of joy!

Who walks in the door in the middle of what we were doing but Peter. His mouth dropped open but, nothing came out. He saw Ole Dude still sniffling and stuff. He said, Ole Dude; if you don't stop crying like a lil B-----!" "Stop it! You better not say that Peter!" Jazzy could barely get the words out of her mouth before a pain hit her that doubled her over! Peter grabbed her and scooped her up in his arms, and headed out of the door. Big Mama was running right behind him to bring her hospital bag. Peter was yelling over his shoulders, "Ole Dude, I'm glad they let you come on home man! That crying woulda got you in some deep sh-- if you stayed up in there any longer!" We all cracked up! Ole Dude did know how to have a good time after all! My little heart was so happy! I still had some apologizing to do though.

Chapter 22

Welcome Home My Friend

There's this feeling that gets to rising up on the inside of you. It annoys you until you "make things right" as Big Mama used to say it. Well, as much as I couldn't stand ole fast tail Janice, I knew that I had to go see her and tell her how I felt. I waited until Jazzy had gone to have the baby so I wouldn't cause her anymore worry, just in case Janice didn't want to act right with me. I had to think of a way to get Big Mama to let me go out to play. She already had our chores lined up for us to do. I ran through my list of chores really fast. I stayed away from Sasha as much as possible. She was on a roll, raising as much hell as possible...with anybody that got in her path. I think she was (in her own way) feeling nervous about this new baby that was coming home in a few days. She may be thinking, for it to take her place in mama's life.

Ever since the Home Going service for JoJo, all of the attention of everyone had been on the crooked cops, Candy Man, and "Ms. Goody Two shoes", Vivian's and Candy Man's mother! All of this time, we were thinking that Vivian was the model child in the neighborhood. Well, you know what we found out? She was the angel in the day and her brother's cohort in the night! She was helping him dog these different baby mamas out on a huge scale! She was not gonna be suspected by the neighborhood parents, or kids. But, she had put the fear of God in the subjects of her brother! She moved his "Candy" for him, forced the girls to "use", and slapped them around when they didn't want to. Bullied them into giving up their government "Issue", basically, she was their "Mack Mama" for Candy Man! Their mom had profited from the loot. So...her mama was basically Pimping Vivian! She didn't claim any of the kids as her grandchildren! When she was greeted in the hood by the mamas with the children, she dismissed them as if they were an embarrassment to her!

Janice was about to be a victim to the hood as well. The baby she was carrying was not Candy Man's. But, it was the grimy officers Gipson...or Ross's baby. They both had had their way with Janice. She was trying to pin it on Teddy. But, JoJo had pulled Teddy's coat tail and showed him how that couldn't even be possible! That's what started the rift between them with the officers. I had a blink of a moment of devilment flash in my mind. I started to think, just for a moment only that; I was doing Janice a favor crashing into her the way that I did. But, the things that I had learned about how God is the giver of life, no matter who's life we feel is not worthy enough...God loves us ALL! So, I quickly dismissed that wicked thought, and set out to find Janice. When I got to the house and knocked at the door, Ole Dude snatched the door open and it scared me so bad, I did a quick spin to run in terror the way that I had come to the house! He grabs me by the collar, and my feet were dangling in midair trying to run! “Lil girl, stop being scared of every little thang!” He was laughing so hard, I couldn't help but start to laughing too. Since I discovered that he did have a soft side, and he had seen my “tuff side” on the field with the boys in the hood; I got bold with him. “Who you calling Lil girl?” He just scooped me by the back of my head with his big hand, and said, “Come on in here Guh.” Janice was in the kitchen, washing dishes. She did something that shocked me. She dried her hands on her clothes, ran over to me, and hugged me so hard and long, that we both were crying with so many mixed emotions! When she finally let me go, all I could do is tell her over and over how sorry I am for making her lose her baby! She held me back by the shoulders and looked me in my eyes, and said, “Sorry? Girl, you don't know how big of a favor you did me!” I was so confused until she told me the “whole” story of how the cops had raped her, and threatened her and Teddy all of that time! She said she didn't know which one of them was the daddy of the baby! I questioned her about not feeling love for the baby. She said the baby was in a better place than coming into this world with the likes of either one of the cops to be its father!

There was still confusion in my heart. Jazzy had always told us that, God had never put a mouth on this planet that he couldn’t feed and take GOOD care of. So, I didn't understand why Janice didn't want her baby. Even if she didn't know who the daddy was...it was surely her baby. There was a saying that, "Mama's Baby, Daddy's maybe." No matter what, the mama carried, and had the baby so; that made it hers! I was really sad for the baby. It was conceived in a savage way, and my pinned up rage slammed it to its death! It never stood a chance. That was the way of life for many in "The Hood". There were many with pinned up rage and hate and confusion, and frustration and such a feeling of defeat and agony for something BETTER! The elderly were "Yet holding on to their faith". I believe that it was the only thing that kept this whole place from exploding into total chaos! There was so much pull and tug on each other! If one person made Popcorn Balls, and the kids flocked to her house too much and spent too much small change with her, some female, that was jealous, called in to report her to "The Man" for making money off of her food stamps! If a woman got a boyfriend in the hood and he had a decent job, the jealous hags with old, good for nothing men turned in the ones that had fresh, new meat to come into their lives! They tried that mess with Jazzy about Peter! You know she went right up in the office and set Mr. Hopkins straight! Peter worked 11pm to 7am most of the time. So, them trying to prove that he stayed overnight with Jazzy was not easy to do. They wanted to regulate who you laid with, who gave you anything and how much, and you sho couldn't have you no side hustle for money! Unless you was Candy Man! Jazzy set them all straight about Peter! By the time she put them on the carpet about how they let Candy Man parade through the hood and sell his "goods" and have these weak minded women selling they bodies and food stamps and giving him they welfare checks; Mr. Hopkins could not even say a word! She says she told them, "If y'all don't get all the way up outta my business I'm gonna get my attorney to sue the pants off of this place for Slander, Harassment and defamation of my character and Peter's!". She still had access to the military family attorney because; she was still legally married to the Military Guy. He just refused to give her a divorce. Then, she went right around to the very ones that had been trying to rat her out! She gave them a piece of her brilliant mind and didn't have to use not one cuss word to get them told all the way off! For somebody that was as pregnant as Jazzy was when this all happened; she had a lot of respect from all of the woman and men in the hood. They knew that she was a woman of dignity. They also knew that it was nothing that she would deny a family if she could help them. They knew that their secrets were safe with her. They knew that Jazzy wasn't going to stand by and watch no child go hungry or not have clothes on their backs and shoes on their feet. Jazzy told this to all of the females that she knew who tried to mess things up for her. All they could do was drop they head and agree with Jazzy. "You right Jazzy. You sho nuff right." She got Mr. Hopkins to see that these women needed these men up in they lives to help them come up and one day get out of the Hood. She showed him how half of the problems with the kids that was wayward was because, they had unhappy mothers and no male guidance. She told him that, "The Man" had been taking the Black man from the home since the days of Slavery! He wanted to know, "What do you expect me to do Jazzy?" "Nothing! Leave us alone and let us live!" He just pointed to the door for her to leave. She did her Jazzy strut right out of the door of his office. She knew that she had gotten through to him. She told the women that she had stuck her neck out for them and they better "Act the Hell right!" She did that for the people in her life and community. She stuck her neck out for the weaker ones; she stuck her neck out for the underdog, those that had less, the hungry, and those that were the outcast of the Hood. But! She was determined to see that, Candy Man and his mammy, (that's what Jazzy called mamas that were bad for their kid's wellbeing) were punished for all of the hurt and ruin they had caused the people in our lives.

Teddy was still away under protective custody. He was the one person that was able to finger all that Vivian's mom had allowed to go on at the hands of her son, while all alone not allowing Vivian's so called "Image" to be tainted. All the while she was using her to "help" Candy Man with these "Problems". She was referring to the baby mamas and the many kids he thought no one could tell was his! You know another thing about growing up in the Hood? These women knew how to look the other way and keep the "who that child daddy" secret right along with the other women that had the same issue in common. Meaning, each one of them knew that their child shared the same dad, Candy Man. But, the code of "Ain't got nothing to do with that child" was the code among all of them! Vivian had these women so spooked that, they didn't dare tell nobody, nothing! But, when her soul got weary of trying to live up to the day to day slime that she was forced to take part in, (if she intended to keep getting money for College that is)... When she could not do the dirt another moment, it was in those moments, she ran to Janice to unload! Janice was her secret keeper. Because, Janice had her own secrets that she needed Vivian to keep. Janice and Teddy's relationship was not so up close and personal after Gipson and Ross got all up in they happenings. They had Teddy under a great squeeze to "Shut up or else", as they slipped through and had their way with Janice. Roxy was in no position to say a word because; they had her right where they wanted her. They let Candy Man bring her "Candy" to her, as she looked the other way. Ole Dude knew if he was there, watching this mess go down, he was gonna be locked away for murdering not one but, two crooked cops! I learned that that is why he walked through with the blank cold stare on his face through the hood some evenings. He had to leave home to keep from facing the cops coming in, violating his Sister, and Candy Man, slithering in on his "Pick up" and "Drop offs" with his Mama! You know, when he sat me down to talk about it all on the stoop that evening that I came over to apologize to Janice; I was not ready for all that came from the heart and mind of this person. He talked to me like I was Jazzy! When he would say stuff that was really "Grown up Stuff", I would try to cover my ears a couple of times. Then, he did something that changed the way I would listen to people from that day on. He stood up and gently took my hands off of my ears and said, "Listen to me please! I need to get this out of my head before I lose my mind Man!" When he called me "Man", I knew he had gone to another place in his head. He was talking as if he needed his Dad to hear his plea for understanding and help! The look he had on his face was so pitiful and desperate all in one instant. I was frozen in the moment. I could not help but, listen to his story, just the way he was telling to me. He wasn't loud, but, furious. He said things that would make a grown man cry about what he had gone through in his life. He just didn't have any tears left for that part of his story. He told it to me almost in a whisper. He just didn't have any more energy to give to it. Knowing that they had been charged with the many crimes that they had committed did him some justice. But, he still had a whole lot of heartache and loneliness that he lived each day. Teddy at least was around to talk to when he would come to hang out with Janice. He said that Teddy was in the same boat as he was. No Dad in his life, a mom that was a victim of Candy Man's poison, and they had Janice in common...who they couldn't help. Despite the rape, and the loss of the baby, Janice walked around every day like nothing got to her, like she was on a "natural high" that was totally a lie! Vivian knew her True self. But, Janice knew hers too....and so did Teddy. He would be over to Janice's every day to get away from the misery in his house! While Janice braided his hair or while he pretended to be reading his comic books, Vivian would be pouring out all of her family problems to Janice. This boasted of how she was paid to dog out them "Dumb Broads" for her Mama and her Brother! But, she would have bad dreams about the kids crying for their daddy, and how she saw faces of their Mamas strung out and looking like dead people coming at her! She told of how hard it was getting to be to keep doing this for the sole purpose of making sure that they never brought none of them "Bastards" to her mama's doorsteps! She told of how Candy Man worked with Gipson to hide him out and help him make his drops by being paid off to look the other way and if he scratched Gipson's back, Gipson would keep his scratched. Janice would just ooo and ahhh and hang on to Vivian's every word as Teddy sat in their company, recalling, days, dates and events that was going to serve to bring down a whole slew of folk! Preachers included! When Gipson got locked up without bail, he quickly started amening to all that Teddy had reported about them! He gave away Candy Man's hide out, told all the dirt on his low down mammy, and Vivian too! They got Vivian for assaulting the many subjects of her brother, plus aiding and abetting, for Pimping and accepting bribes to do it. Do you know at the last, Vivian tried to take Janice and Roxy down with her to get a lighter sentence! Because, Janice listened to her vent and share her and her brother's dirty deeds, she felt like she ought to be punished for not saying anything! I was wondering what kind of fool she thought Janice really was?! She had already been raped and had a second attempt of it on the school yard by Ross! I know she was hot in the draws but, I would at least want to have the say about who I let in my draws! Nadine had taught us that much.

Chapter 23

"Lord, Don't Take Cinnamon Too!"

****

Jazzy had that baby! Finally! We waited for an eternity it seemed for her to get home with the baby! She was a Red and wrinkled little thang! She was very little, and cried a whole lot, night and day! It was taking a toll on all of us! Except Miriam that is. She acted just like it didn't bother her at all! She wanted to help warm the bottle for her and help give her a bath and hold her when she was screaming to the top of her lungs! It didn't matter. She just wanted to be around this child! Jazzy and Peter were both exhausted by the time they got home with her. It helped them that Miriam could help out with the baby. Miriam didn't even want us to get too close up on the baby! She said we could take the baby's breath away by breathing to close to her face. She even showed us the baby's "Soft Spot"! It was moving when you looked at it really good! "Wow!" She said that we should Never touch her head right there! She said if we mashed it too hard right there, she could die! Of course, old mean tail Sasha didn't believe it and told her so. Miriam just told her, "You heard what I said". We knew that tone too well. Oh yeah! I almost forgot to tell y'all the baby's name! I guess they took in to account that she was such a dusty red headed little ole thang. So, they say they both agreed that her name should be "Cinnamon". Sasha wanted to know, "What kind of crazy name is that?" Miriam, me and Malcolm rather liked it! Malcolm would not even touch her! When Jazzy tried to let him hold her, he was not having it. He told mama that he was scared of babies when they were that size. He said that they looked "Strange". Sasha looked bright eyed when she first saw her. But, after that, we would catch her over in a corner or posted up with her thumb in her mouth somewhere rolling her eyes at this innocent baby! Jazzy told her that the baby made her a "New Big Sister" now. She said, "I ain't finna be combing and washing her hair or nothing!" Jazzy asked her why she said it like that. She said, "Because, all Miriam do is pop me and Monia on the top of our head with that brush when we can't hold our head the right way! She just said that we can't be touching that baby "Soft Spot" or else she will die! I ain't getting no whipping for nobody about that little red, ugly baby!" She stuck her thumb in her mouth and started banging her back up against the couch, back and forth and back and forth. We fell out! Peter laughed so hard he had tears running down his face! Malcolm hadn't ever laughed that hard. Sasha didn't crack one smile.

The days of summer were so steamy and hot. The mosquitos were so mean in the south! It was like they were on a mission to win the contest of which could sting the most and which could bite the hardest! They bit you so fast and got away so fast, you would just be slapping and popping your arm and leg and head and back for nothing! Because, when you looked at your hand to see if you got it....nothing was there! Nobody in our house could stand the heat! Mama and Cinnamon had on as few clothes as possible when she was nursing her. Peter would never disrespect us by going around the house with his shirt off. Jazzy got that straight with him when he first came to stay the night over. They were in Jazzy's bedroom with the door closed. He had to go use the bathroom. He was just going to come out with his pants and house slippers on, and go straight across to the bathroom. You could hear from one room to the other because they were all right there together. We were already in our rooms for the night just reading and coloring in our books. When Peter turned the knob to come out of the room, Jazzy asked him, "Where the hell do you think you going with no shirt on through my house?" He said, "I told you that I had to use the bathroom Jazzy.". She said, "You certainly don't think that you gonna walk around my girls with that kind of disrespect do you Peter? That is not gonna go on up in here! I don't know what kind of arrangements you and Etta had going on, but not in front of my girls!" "Oh so, they Yo girls now huh Jazzy?" He grabbed his shirt, threw it on really fast, headed to the bathroom and slammed the door! Jazzy yelled, "And don't be slamming my doors either!" We all got quiet, Malcolm came out of his room and wanted to know was Mama alright. Because, we had not heard her act this way with Peter since the time around Christmas when Mama was mad because, Etta was trying to play them games that she said baby mama's did when the man had found another woman. Peter was the one doing most of the fussing then though, and it was about Jazzy allowing Etta to get "under her skin". We had not seen Jazzy act this way with Peter. Everybody was still being happy about Cinnamon. We was just HOT! It seemed like the heat was making everybody act up! Mama made us stay in from football for a while because, there were too many fights breaking out among us. Very few people had been hanging outside during the day. Some of the men would come out at night and put old clothes and scraps in these tin foot tubs or old pots and burn them to keep the mosquitos at bay they said. They would be out there drinking they beer, and playing the Blues and Lying! That's what Big Mama said they be doing anyway. Well, Jazzy told Malcolm to go on back in his room, and that nothing was wrong. Peter came out of the bathroom and walked back to Jazzy's room and grabbed his cigarettes, stormed to the kitchen to get a beer, and headed out the back door, and slammed that one too! Jazzy told Miriam to come in her room, and stay with Cinnamon for a minute. Me and Sasha got nervous. We knew that look in our Mama's eyes. Sasha started welling up and pacing with her thumb in her mouth and tears of fear in her eyes. Malcolm didn't stay in the room like Jazzy had said. He came out and followed her towards the kitchen door, right on her heels. Miriam told us to come in there with her and Cinnamon. We were getting scared. We all knew that our mama would fight in a heartbeat! We just loved Peter so much; we didn't want her to fight him. We heard him saying, "Gone back in yo house with yo children Jazzy. Ain't no women out here no way. Gone now Jazzy. I just want to sit out here and drank my beer in peace. Just gone in there with yo baby Jazzy.". He must've put his hand on her to get her to come on back in the house. I heard Malcolm say, "Nawww man, you can't do that. Come on Ma. You just had that baby in there. You got to let this one slide. Come on back in the house Jazzy." "Peter! You got to come back in this house!" Jazzy made it clear that she would be laying in the cut for him! Miriam told us to go on back in our room before Jazzy got back in the house. Cinnamon started crying so loud! It was as if, she knew that there was trouble in the house...

Jazzy was just walking the floor, puffing on them stanky cigarettes! I asked her very timidly, "Mama, (not calling her Jazzy so she could remember she was a new mama now) I think that your cigarette smoke might be bothering the baby, she seem like it's hard for her to breath and she's turning redder in there.". Mama turned around so fast that she just dropped the cigarette on the floor and ran in the room to see what I was talking about! Miriam was just rocking her and crying silent tears. We knew when Jazzy had gotten on "One", we needed to stir clear of her until it passed! She reached down and took Cinnamon from Miriam's arms and held her out in front of her and looked at her, and started running with her towards the back door, screaming, "Peter! Get the car! Something's wrong with Cinnamon!" She didn't wait on him because; he thought that she was just trying to get him to come back in the house. "Miriam, call Patsy! Tell her to come over here now! Call Big Mama and tell her to PRAY! Monia, get that Diaper bag and my wig, and come with me!" I knew when she told me to come on and go with her, that meant that she needed me to be her shadow and to do whatever she said, and don't speak unless she asked me something. This was what she always did in those times. She wanted to speak some matters of the heart as she was driving...really fast! I kept my eyes on Cinnamon, and was praying under my breath as Mama was talking to me and driving. "Lord Jesus, you gave us this baby. And, if you let her die now, Mrs. Tyler is going to believe she was right, and she would think that you did it because, Jazzy wouldn't give me to her, so you took Cinnamon from Peter and Jazzy to show them that your blessing is not on their Love. Dear Lord, Dummy is gone, JoJo is gone. Please Lord don't take Cinnamon from us too! Jesus, we need her in our life, Veronica nem haven't even seen her yet! Please Lord, Fix it! I love you Jesus. Thank you for saving Cinnamon.". Jazzy must've heard me praying because, she stopped talking to me. By that time we were at the hospital emergency room. Patsy had called to tell them we were coming with the baby. They met us out at the car and took her and started running with her. They put a little thing on her face that Jazzy said would help her breath. She parked the car and we ran inside to go find Cinnamon. They tried to make Jazzy leave me out of the room. She told them that there was nobody to leave me with so that I could stay by her side. She always pulled me close to her like she got some sort of strength or something from me being with her. I know that God heard my prayer because; pretty soon they told us that we could come be with Cinnamon. I tapped Jazzy on her arm and whispered in her ear, "Jazzy, you can't smoke those cigarettes around Cinnamon no more." She just looked me in the eyes and said, "you know what Monia, You are so right!' When she saw Cinnamon, she broke down in tears and was just rubbing on every part of her little body like; she wanted to touch every part to make sure it was okay. The doctor told Jazzy that, "She was going to have to stop breastfeeding Cinnamon if she was going to continue to smoke cigarettes. Or, she could quit smoking cigarettes. It was up to her." She didn't have to think too hard about it at all. They hadn't left the room before Peter ran up in the room. He ran straight past all of us to go to Cinnamon. They told him to let her rest, her lungs had been through a lot, and they wanted her to rest. They asked if he smoked too. He told them he did. They told him the same thing they had told Jazzy. He looked at Jazzy and said, "Done". They told us that they would check back in a bit and they felt that she should be able to go home in a little while. They told us that she would need to have breathing treatments with this thing they gave them to bring home. But, the smoking would definitely have to stop. I sat in the back of the car silently crying tears of joy and telling the Lord "Thank you Jesus for answering our prayer to save Cinnamon." I knew that more than me was praying for her and about Peter and Jazzy too. Because, when they were at the hospital, they were hugging and crying together and apologizing to each other for things that lead them to that place in the first place. I was so happy because, I needed Peter to stay in my life and Cinnamon really needed him too.

When we got home with Cinnamon, guess who was on the porch? Ole Dude! I wondered how he heard about Cinnamon. He said, "I was out there talking to Peter when it all happened." Unbeknownst to us, Ole Dude had his eye on Miriam! That's right. He was down there to have a talk with Peter to see if he thought Jazzy would be okay with him "Rapping with" Miriam sometimes. He was doing his usual stroll. But, he would walk after dark because of the heat. I told him to come on in out of the Mosquitos! Big Mama lit up when she saw us come in from the hospital. She went straight for Cinnamon. She gave orders to Jazzy to go lay her tail down and get some rest! She held Cinnamon liked a football cradled in the bend of her arm as she moved around the room giving orders to all of us. She made Patsy, "Go in there and make sho Jazzy doing what I said. She done had enough excitement for one day. She gone mess around and have a "Set back" if sheen careful! Trying to have her way with Peter and tryna fight and carry on! I don't know where she gets these ole feisty ways from!" We all sang out in unison, "Big Mama!" She just held Cinnamon up to her nose and smelled that sweet baby aroma and held her up toward the ceiling and said, "Lawd, you gonna have to help us with this one! Between that Peter being stubbon as a mule, and talking slow as the dickens, and Jazzy being all of the different ways she is, Lawd if you don't keep yo hands on this child, I don't thank the world gonna be able to handle huh! You done already gave us a sign Lawd with this Red all over huh from head to toe! Help us Jesus!" We all laughed. But, we knew that there was some seriousness to every word she said. Ole Dude was laughing heartily along with us and you could see Miriam looking at him with a blush on her face. I never would've thunk it! But, I liked it! Now I could have both of my two favorite people around, teenagers that is. Me and Big Mama both saw the exchange between them. We just gave each other that knowing look that we gave each other sometimes. Miriam was grinning from ear to ear! While they were all laughing and Peter had calmed down too, I pulled him by the arm and asked if I could talk to him about something before he went to bed. He gave a, "What 21 questions you got for me now Monia?" kind of look. I just laughed and pushed him toward the door so we could talk away from the others. "Peter, I know Jazzy said that we were "Her Girls" But, I just wanted you to know that, I feel like we are Your Girls too! Please don't believe what she is saying right now. She seems like something is bothering her right now. But, I don't think it's you though. It could be Mrs. Tyler, Nadine, or missing JoJo or Dummy. It could be that she wants to be divorced from that Military Guy, so she can be yo wife. I don't know what it is. But, I know she loves you being with us, and she don't want you to go. So, please don't go" "Monia, I have a question for you. Why do you call your dad, "That Military Guy?" I had to wonder why he gave any thought to that, over everything else that I just said to him. "I don't want to talk about him. I want to make sure that you don't leave just like he did. You don't treat me the way that he did." "How is that?" "It makes my stomach hurt when I think about it. So, can we please not talk about him?" "Does Jazzy know that it makes you feel like that when you think about him?" "I don't know, she never talks about him to me." "Is it only you?" "Malcolm either." "Hmmm, is that right?" "Yep." "Well, we just need to see about that." "No!" He caught me by the shoulders, and tried to calm me down. "Monia, it's okay! We don't have to talk about it if you don't want to right now." I told him that I didn't ever want to talk about him again! He put his arm around my shoulder and said, "Come on, let's go inside, I ain't going No

Where!" I just hung on to his belt and walk with a Big and Happy feeling in my chest and a feeling that I could go to bed now and really sleep good! I was so drained in my soul for one day! Nosy Sasha wanted to know what I had to talk about with Peter. I told her that I wanted to make sure that him and Jazzy was gonna really stop all of that smoking around Cinnamon like the doctor told them to do. She said, "I ain't gonna stop sucking my thumb and they ain't gonna stop sucking on them stanky cigarettes because of that ugly red baby coming here!" I was too weak to even argue with her. I was certainly too weak to fight her that night before bed. I didn't need that sleeping pill at all! I heard Big Mama getting ready to go to bed on the sofa bed. She just marched in the living room and said, "Ole Dude, go home. You done grinned up in Miriam face enough already. Um tied and ret to lay these bones down for the day. Jazzy done got the whole neighborhood stirred up about huh guhs and that little Red tail baby in nair!"

The next morning, it wasn't Cinnamon's crying that woke us up, It was Jazzy and Big Mama yelling praises to God for them finally catching up with Candy Man! Vivian couldn't take being locked up and being beat up and dogged out by the other inmates. She told the D.A. all that he had done. This was totally in line with what Teddy had told them! This got her mama locked up...who thought she was home free. She was willing to let her daughter take the fall so she could go free! That was certainly the opposite of what God did! He gave his Only Son so that we could go free! They sent the Special Unit boys out to get her and Candy Man! The commotion that was going on outside was like there was a Block party, early in the morning in New Roads Projects! All of the women that had been tormented and dejected, and suppressed and oppressed at the hands of these two gangstas was finally over...but, not quite over. Their kids were left Fatherless, they had to rely on any help that they could get from the County, and no one had much respect for them because, they let Candy Man do them that way. Even I knew that when the devil came into your life, his grip has a hold on you that's very hard to get off of you! My struggle wasn't theirs. But, I knew that I had something going on within me that I knew that it would take the power of Jesus to help me get free! You see, Cinnamon showed me something about Innocence. From the time she was just 6 months old, she knew what to do to get Jazzy to pick her up or let her have her way with her! At 6 months old, she knew what it meant when you told her to, "Stop", or "No". She didn't like being told "No", She would squall like she was being beaten to get her way! I saw how "Manipulation" caused a whirlwind of problems for people at the last. Vivian was taught very well to manipulate people! But, she became a victim of her own doing! Big Mama said she felt sorry for her, and was going to go down and see if she could plead with the DA for her to be given a lighter charge. She was concerned that Vivian was a smart girl and didn't deserve to be locked up and beaten up by all of those hard women up in there. Jazzy reminded her that, that was what she had done to all of the other women out here in the hood!" Big Mama's argument was that, "This child had a plan to go to College and be somebody!" Jazzy said, "She's already somebody! These girls out here deserved just as much of a chance as Vivian did Big Mama! They had a chance to do something great in life! Now, they are stuck with these babies and their whole estimate of life and their value to contribute to life don't mean Shit in their eyes Big Mama! “Watch yo mouth there now Jazzy!" "I'm sorry Big Mama, I just got carried away. I am so tired of seeing these women, with sadness and despair in their eyes; I'm tired of seeing these kids looking for someone to make some sense of it all...Even Monia!" “What you mean Monia?" "Yes. Monia, she has been going through the same thing! Wondering why there is so much Hurt, and Disappointment and Despair in "The Hood?" What's to become of the people down in this part of the Parish?" Big Mama looked at me with an empty look in her eyes. She didn't know that I was going through that struggle. She simply said, "Monia, what you pose we need to do about this?" "Big Mama, I think we need to go find Dave, and let him know we still got love for him, and we need to find Nadine, and let her know that we ain't mad at here no more, and, Mrs. Tyler too. We need to get Veronica and Jessica over here and let them be in Cinnamon's life and even if Etta wants to come see Cinnamon, it ought"..."Monia, you asking a whole lot of me!" Jazzy was not ready to trust Etta with Cinnamon just yet. She said that she barely did right by her own girls! We just laughed a little. But, we all saw that look in Jazzy's eyes that let us know that she was about to get on one of her "Missions". Let's just say, New Roads was about to get a Heart and Mind transplant according to Jazzy Jones…

I hadn't spent much time at all in my tree. The summer days were hot and the Crepe had blossomed with the beautiful clusters of flowers and their buds. We used to pick the buds off of the flowers before they opened and we would squeeze the flowers out of them before they had a chance to sprout out. We would use the buds as ammo to have a Pellet war with each other. Malcolm was the best at it! He could really sting you when he sent a bud flying in the air at you! I really miss those days in New Roads. Life was different then. We struggled, and lived a life that most would look down on. But, I learned about Pride, and Integrity, and Respect in the Hood. I learned how to Love in the Hood. I learned what true friendship meant from the lessons I got in the Hood. I learned to lean and depend on Jesus in the Hood. There was heartache there, there was also sharing and caring there. As I look back on the times that that part of my journey brought about in my life, I have no regrets. The Tylers came back around and apologized....even Jeremy. Of course Mrs. T found it hard to give Cinnamon back to Jazzy to put her down to nap. Jazzy had to almost pry Cinnamon from her arms. Nadine came back around and of course you know that her pride tried to make it seem like she had been doing good without us in her life for that little stretch of time. She was so full of herself! Get this! We discovered that Dave had founded a Church fellowship on the other side of the river from us! He was preaching for Jesus now! Guess who was a member at his church? Yes! Nadine! Big Mama said, "If Nadine done took her crazy tail up in somebody's chuch to serve the Lawd, then, it's time for us all to get right with God and get on back in the House of Prayer!"

Thank you for letting me share my story with you. Or, was it Jazzy's story? Lord you know....and so does Myrtle.

END

If you have enjoyed "Lord You Know, and So Does Myrtle", keep your eyes opened for "Flowers in the Ghetto"!

"Lord You Know, and So Does Myrtle"

Chapter 1

Could It Be The Poppies?

They were never allowed to come past the corner to play with any of the kids on their block. They wore dresses every day. Their grandma was raising them because their Mom abandoned them to be "A lady of the Night" out in Cali somewhere. We would try to find excuses to go down to Aunt Maggie's so we could get a closer look at these strange girls. Sometimes they would be out on the raggedy sidewalk in front of their granny's, and they would have pieces of stuff that was like the stuff we stashed away in the junk drawer in the kitchen at our house. They would have a top to a jar, or rubber bands, or a piece of string or twine. The way they played with these odd objects made it seem like they had just gotten them for gifts at Christmas time! They would jump around in laughter and glee as if they were in a field of Sunflowers in some strange euphoria! Aunt Maggie told us that we better not dare make fun of them! She said that they were different from us "Ingrates"! She said, "They are grateful for the 'little things' in life". She was certainly right about that! I needed to get closer to them to find out why….

Nina was always on to some sort of wild, hot news that none of us had ever heard of! She came running like the Town Crier to tell us of her grand discovery of what could possibly be making Rebecca and Hanna; (the weird sisters) act like they were on cloud 9. She fell upon us, all out of breath. Her eyes looked like they would bulge out of their sockets! “Y’all ain’t gonna believe it! Y’all ain’t gonna believe it!” “Believe what?” we kept asking her. “Them girls’ granny been putting them on “That Lady”! That's why they act like that!”. “What lady?” We asked in unison. “Not what lady fools! “That Lady” is what the drug is that she been giving them po girls! It’s that white powder stuff that we saw Bubba nem putting in they nose. Then, they start acting all strange and goofy and stuff. At least Bubba gets giggly. Doug always wants to fight or start up some mess with somebody. Don’t he y’all?” I was still looking at her real crazy for trying to make us believe that that sweet old lady would be making her grandbabies take drugs of any kind! Juanita told Nina, “Go on somewhere with that crazy mess you talkin! Ain’t nobody trying to hear that!” I was still looking at her like she was crazy. She went on to make her case. “Y’all know how they said, “They mama went off and left them, running behind some man?” Well, that really messed up that oldest girl’s mind. Rebecca I think they say her name is.”. “Who is ‘they’ anyway Guh?” I had to know where she was getting her information from. “Don’t worry about where I get my goods from.” She said with much false dignity. You have to know Nina well. She needs to feel like she has the juiciest news of the whole bunch. I don’t know anybody that can embellish, and lie like Nina….except one other person...Old man Stewart! That dude can liiieee! I’m just about ready to connect the two of them together in this nonsense!

Stewart lives right on the line of the city side of the ghetto, and far enough on the rural side to get the low down on both! He didn’t want the positive and praise worthy stuff to talk about from either side! He prided himself on the fact that people flocked over to his yard to sit under the tree in his yard to get the skinny on everybody he knew, and all of those he didn’t know…but, was gonna make it his business to know some dirt on them! It's a shame because he gossiped worse than the women around town! He didn't even have no shame about it either! What's so sad is that he's the oldest person around that side of town and he has seen the past of those that have gone on to their destination, and have family that loved them and still do. He didn't care though. He would dig up stuff from the grave on them! Stuff that God had already forgiven mind you. He knew all of the real daddies and the "that's who they say" daddies were to all of the children here and there, let him tell it! He ***kept*** the women stirred up against each other!

Stephanie Hart

My Mainstays

These Scriptures are not used in the story. But, they are just a few that are Mainstays that give me hope and strength. They have comforted me, and reminded me of WHO I am, and WHOSE I am, and the purpose for my being. They have kept me humble; lest I forget.

(1 Peter 2: 9-10)
(Psalm 23)
(Psalm 121)
(Psalm 116)
(Acts 17:28)
(John 15:5)
Amen

All Scriptures were taken from the King James Version of the Holy Bible unless noted otherwise.

Made in the USA
Columbia, SC
23 April 2025